REPORT TO THE PRINCIPAL'S OFFICE

Report to the Principal's Office

Who Ran My Underwear Up the Flagpole?

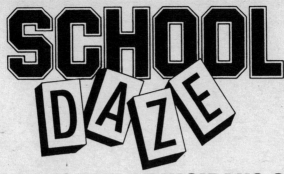

REPORT TO THE PRINCIPAL'S OFFICE

JERRY SPINELLI

Newbery-award-winning author
of *Maniac Magee*

AN
APPLE
PAPERBACK

SCHOLASTIC INC.
New York Toronto London Auckland Sydney

ISBN 0-590-44402-6

12 11 10 9 8 7 6 5 4 3 2   1 2 3 4 5 6/9

Printed in the U.S.A.   40

First Scholastic printing, October 1991

Thank yous are in order to the following contributors to this book:
Pat Carbone, teacher; Judy Anderson, teacher; and Jennie Singleton, kid.

For Sherwood and Rowena Mercer
Marion Baker
and Mardie Bell

1

Sunny Wyler opened her front door and stepped out of her house. Directly across the street, Hillary Kain came out of her house. The instant the two best friends saw each other, they burst into tears.

They met on the sidewalk in front of Sunny's house.

"Come on," sniffed Hillary, "I'll walk you to the bus."

They walked as slowly as they could.

"Look at this," said Sunny, picking at the sleeve of her DEATH TO MUSHROOMS T-shirt. "Same rag I wore last year. I'm gonna wear it every day till we're back together again."

"Won't you have to get it washed?"

"I'm not gonna."

"You'll start to smell."

"Good," grumbled Sunny. "The worse I smell, the faster they'll kick me out and transfer me to your school."

1

"Now I feel guilty," said Hillary.

"Why?"

"Here I am with my new clothes. I should give up more, like you."

"Don't be a moron," said Sunny. "You know me. I overdo everything. You're doing the hair. That's enough."

"You think so?"

"I think so."

The girls had vowed that from that day forward, they would never again wash their hair till they were back in the same school.

For seven years — preschool, kindergarten, grades one through five — Sunny and Hillary had gone to the same school. In fact, at Drumore Elementary, they had always shared the same classroom. They became best friends. They went on vacations with each others' families. And to top it off, they lived directly across the street from each other. They were meant to be together. Nothing would ever break them up.

But something did.

Two sinister forces were at work during those seven years. One force was population movement. More and more families were making their homes in Cedar Grove.

The other force was babies. People were having more of them than before. Newspapers called it the "Baby Boomlet." Even so, babies alone were not the problem. The problem was, they got older.

The problem was, sooner or later the babies became sixth-graders.

The problem was, Cedar Grove Middle School could not hold them all.

The *problem* was, they built a new middle school — Plumstead — to hold the growing population.

The PROBLEM was, when they drew the line on the town map to decide who goes to Cedar Grove and who goes to Plumstead, they drew it smack dab down the middle of the street that Sunny Wyler and Hillary Kain lived on.

Hillary would go to the old school, Cedar Grove. Sunny would go to the new one, Plumstead.

"I feel like I'm walking to the gallows," said Sunny.

"Me, too," said Hillary. She fished around for something helpful to say. "Look on the bright side. You're going to a brand-new school. New desks, new everything. I hear they even have air-conditioning."

"I don't *want* air-conditioning," Sunny grumped. "I just want to go to Cedar Grove."

They looked at each other. More tears came. And, in the case of Sunny, something else.

"Your nose is running," said Hillary.

Sunny sniffed. The runner retreated like a turtle's head.

"It's the baby boomlet's fault," said Hillary.

"It's our parents' fault," said Sunny. "The rats."

3

Hillary nodded. It was true. Their very own parents had been among the worst offenders of the boomlet. Each girl had two younger siblings — Sunny, two brothers, and Hillary, a brother and sister.

"We should've stopped them," Sunny said. "We should've put our foot down. 'No more babies.' "

"Then you wouldn't have any little brothers," Hillary pointed out.

A wicked grin curled Sunny's lip. "Yeah, too bad." Little brothers were not Sunny's favorite people.

"Your nose again," said Hillary.

This time Sunny did not sniff. "Let it run. I'm never gonna wipe it. I'm not gonna smile. I'm not gonna talk, not even if a teacher asks me a question. They'll be so disgusted with me and my bad attitude and my stinky shirt and my greasy hair, they'll *have* to transfer me. They'll *beg* me to go. They'll hire a limo to take me away."

If anyone else had said this, Hillary would have cracked up. But she knew her friend was perfectly serious and in no mood to be laughed at.

"We're here," said Hillary.

Sunny walked on. "I think it's the next corner." If she could only keep walking, she would never be there, it would never happen.

"Sunny," called Hillary, "*this* is the corner."

Sunny stopped. She slumped, beaten. A sigh of

utter desolation rose from her heart. She returned to Hillary.

The two friends stood grimly, silently, by the stop sign. Two blocks away, a yellow bus turned onto the street. Suddenly Sunny felt emptied of everything inside. She grabbed onto Hillary and felt Hillary squeeze back.

The bus should have come slowly, creeping, respecting her feelings. Instead, it roared to the curbside and, without the slightest hesitation, flung open its door.

"Oh," peeped Sunny.

The two friends hugged, inches from the yawning door. Sunny did not notice, but Hillary's hug was slightly lopsided. As much as she loved Sunny, Hillary did not care to have her new shirt become a handkerchief for Sunny's runny nose.

"Let's go, girls," called the bus driver. "I got a lotta people to pick up."

Sunny wasn't surprised at the remark. She had already decided that the Plumstead bus drivers would be despicable gorillas.

She parted from Hillary, mounted the steps, and before she could wave to her friend, the door had shut, and the bus was roaring away. Okay, she thought, one final word before I shut up forever. She paused beside the bus driver. Sure enough, there was hair growing out of his ears. "Gorilla," she said, and walked down the aisle.

2

Eddie Mott watched the girl come down the aisle with a growing dread. The seat next to him was empty. He had been hoping it would be filled by someone friendly and talkative, someone who would help take his mind off the fact that this was his first day of middle school.

But the girl looked anything but friendly. He had seen her glare at the bus driver and say something to him. Now, as she came nearer, he got a full view of the scowl on her face. It was worse than anything he had ever seen on a TV wrestler. And then he spotted the gleam under her left nostril.

This girl's got problems, he thought. Please don't let her sit here.

But sit there she did. Plopped herself right down next to him, scowling straight ahead.

Up till now, things had gone about as well as could be expected. Eddie had been determined to break the bonds of little boyhood and take that first big step into a more grown-up world. Every school day for five years, his mother had walked him to Brockhurst Elementary. But last night he had said, "Mom, I want to walk to the bus myself." And he had.

He had picked out his own clothes to wear. Middle school clothes. The Daffy Duck pin that he had worn every day last year lay back in his bedroom dresser.

Leaving his memories behind was not so easy. At just about this time of the morning every day last year, he and Roger Himes would be raising the American flag outside Brockhurst. That had been his job all through fifth grade.

But now he was a sixth-grader, and doggonnit, he was going to fit in. That's why he had made up a three-point plan:

1. Be friendly.
2. Wear the right clothes.
3. Avoid eighth-graders.

The last point was advice from Roger Himes, whose older brother was now entering high school. "Stay away from eighth-graders," warned Roger. "They'll get you in trouble. They run the school."

Things had been going well until the sourpussed girl plopped down beside him. Now he began to feel his control of the situation slipping away. All morning he had been wearing an especially friendly face. If only she would turn and see how friendly he was . . .

"Hi," he said.

The girl didn't move an inch. She continued to stare glumly at the back of the seat in front of her.

Maybe she has a hearing problem, he thought. He couldn't see a hearing aid. Maybe it was in the ear on the side away from him.

So this time he tapped her lightly on the wrist when he said it: "Hi."

Still she didn't move. Was she hypnotized? In a trance?

The half of her face that he could see was the side with the running nostril. Actually, it wasn't running at all. It was simply sitting there, a gleaming little puddle, as though it had just crept out to have a look around. And it was really starting to bother him, Eddie being a very neat kid. It was all he could do to keep from whipping out his hankie and wiping it away. Maybe if he brought it to her attention in a nice way. . . .

"Got a cold there?" he said as pleasantly as possible.

Slowly the girl's head turned — he had never seen a head turn so slowly — till she was fully facing him. He froze. She raised her upper lip till she looked like a snarling Doberman. She sniffed.

The gleamer zipped back into her nose. She turned away.

Eddie allowed himself a breath. Now that the first move was over, he decided it hadn't really been so bad. After all, she did turn, she did respond to him. Must have been his friendly face. Maybe he should say something a little meatier this time.

"I hear the new school has air-conditioning," he said.

Again the head slowly turned. The girl spoke. "The next person that tells me the new school has air-conditioning is gonna get a punch in the face."

For the rest of the ride, Eddie looked out the window.

When the bus arrived at school, Eddie made sure to let the grump get well ahead of him. It was slow going down the aisle, as the bus had been filled to the gills. Eddie was scrunched front and back. He held his lunch bag to his chest. Everybody towered over him.

There was a commotion up front, bringing the aisle to a standstill. Kids up front were yelling to kids in back — all eighth-graders, no doubt. The kids up front were calling for their football. The kids in back were saying they didn't have it. The kids up front said they weren't getting off till they got it. The bus driver was calling them all delinquents and telling them to get off his bus, he had a job to get to.

"Throw the ball!" yelled the guys up front.

"Okay," yelled the guys behind, "you asked for it!" And suddenly Eddie was off his feet, hands under him from ankles to shoulders. He was horizontal, on his back, staring straight up at the white ceiling of the bus. "Here!" yelled the voices below him, and he was flying — *flying!* — down the aisle — *above* the aisle — clutching his lunch bag, landing in a squirmy bed of hands.

"Hey," yelled the new voices, "*this* ain't our ball!" And he was flying back down the aisle. At that point, the bus driver went totally wacko and started tossing kids off the bus.

When Eddie came to his senses, he found himself alone on the backseat.

3

T. Charles Brimlow was as ready as he would ever be. Fifteen minutes before the first bus arrived, he was out front wearing a smile as wide as his bow tie. And why not? He was a brand-new principal in a brand-new school. Talk about a fresh start! And he was determined to make the most of it.

The town, the architects, the taxpayers — they had given him all any principal could ask for in the way of a facility. The most modern this, the most up-to-date that. High-tech electronics from boiler room to kitchen. But without people, it was just a brick-and-glass skeleton. Students, teachers, staff — they would bring it to life, give it heart and soul.

And it was he — T. Charles Brimlow — more than any other person, who would determine the quality, the character of that heart and soul. He could only be successful, he had decided, if he and the students worked together as a team. Or even better, as a family. That was the key word: family. He intended to keep that word constantly in mind as he guided these 340 kids through their three years at Plumstead.

All summer long Mr. Brimlow had studied their records and profiles and pictures, so that now, beaming as the buses began to arrive, he felt as if he already knew them. It was a stitch, watching the surprise on the kids' faces as he held out his hand and greeted many of them by name.

"Good morning, Jennifer. Welcome to Plumstead."

"Hiya, Robert. You look like you've gained weight over the summer."

"Morning, Claudia. Still want to be a pilot?"

Now here was a dark-haired girl he couldn't place. Of course, that might be because her face was contorted into one of the most miserable frowns he had ever seen. He felt an instant need to make this child happy.

"Hello, there," he said cheerfully. "I'm Mister Brimlow. What's your name?"

"Butthead," replied the girl and breezed on past.

By the time Mr. Brimlow recovered, the girl was long gone and another stood in front of him. This one had long, curly hair, a thin, interesting face, and large eyes that seemed on the verge of astonishment. Slung over her shoulder was a green book bag. Her name was about to come to him, but she was first to speak. "You're Mister Brimlow, aren't you?"

"I am," he said, still somewhat dazed by the first girl.

"The principal?"

"So they tell me."

She smiled broadly and thrust out her hand. "Nice to meet you. I'm Salem Brownmiller."

He shook her hand. "Salem *Jane* Brownmiller, to be exact."

Her wide eyes widened. "You *know* me?"

"I know your school profile."

She sagged a trifle — "Oh" — then perked up again. "So you know I'm a writer."

"Indeed I do. You won the story contest at Hillmont last year."

She beamed. "I won a gold pin. The story was called 'The Squirrels of Pauline.' It's about this fifth-grade girl and two baby squirrels she meets when lightning strikes a tree in the playground and they fall from their nest. Would you like to read it?"

"I certainly would," replied the principal.

In a flash the girl whipped out some stapled sheets from her book bag and thrust them into his hand. "I carry copies of my stories everywhere I go. You never know when somebody might ask for one. Or suppose my house burns down with all my manuscripts in it!"

Mr. Brimlow was considering the horror of it

13

when a short, portly man with hair in his ears tapped him on the shoulder. "You the bus monitor?"

"No, I'm the principal. Can I help you?"

"Yeah," said the portly man. "I got a kid here won't get off my bus."

4

The mashed stump of a cigar moved about the mouth of the portly, hairy-eared man as though it had a life of its own. "I could drag the kid off," he went on, "but I don't need to get sued. I already put my hands on enough of 'em. In ten minutes I gotta be to the gas station. This ain't my only job, chief."

Mr. Brimlow nodded. "Lead the way."

Salem Brownmiller tugged on his sleeve. "Oh, Mr. Brimlow, can I come, too? I'm writing a story about a girl's first day in middle school, and this could make a really neat subplot."

The principal faced her sternly. "Miss Brownmiller, whoever that is in the bus, it is a person, not a subplot."

For once, the girl was slow to speak. Those wide eyes stared up at him. "I didn't mean it that way, Mr. Brimlow."

The principal softened. "All right. Keep your distance, and don't interfere."

The boy was in the backseat of the bus. His head was slightly atilt. A brown lunch bag rested on his lap, held by both hands. The toes of his new sneakers pointed toward each other. They did not reach the floor.

The principal walked halfway down the aisle and stopped. The boy seemed to be staring at a point in space, about a foot in front of his own face. Mr. Brimlow remembered the face . . . Brockhurst . . .

"Edward?" he said gently. In the background the first bell rang. Students yelped, streamed past the bus windows. "Edward Mott?"

No response.

"Brockhurst? . . . Flag boy?"

Edward Mott's head remained still, but his eyes rolled upward.

"I'm Mister Brimlow, your new principal." He sat on the edge of a seat. "Would you like to come up here and sit with me?"

No answer.

The principal moved one seat closer. "You know, Edward — do your friends call you Eddie?" The boy shrugged. "You know, Eddie, we have something in common, you and I. Can you guess what it is?"

Eddie Mott shrugged.

"Well, I'll tell you. This is *your* first day as a sixth-grader, and it's *my* first day as principal. How about that?"

The answer came from the front of the bus. "I don't get outta here, this is my *last* day at the station. There's a mechanic down there can't work on cars 'cause he gotta pump *gas* because *I* ain't there to pump gas."

Mr. Brimlow stood. He clapped his hands. "Okay, Eddie, what do you say? Ready to go?"

Eddie Mott finally spoke: "No."

"That does it," growled the driver. The door swung shut, the engine rumbled to life, the bus lurched down the driveway.

"Hey!" said Principal Brimlow.

"We're being hijacked!" piped Salem Brownmiller, not unhappily.

The bus roared right on past the school bus parking lot and did not stop till it humped up to the restroom of the Texaco station on the corner of Grant and Mudd.

The driver flipped his hand as he jumped off. "You wanna fire me, fire me."

It was now 8:10 A.M., ten minutes into the first period of the first day at Plumstead Middle School, and a lot of people didn't know where a lot of things were. The gym teachers couldn't find a foot-

17

ball, the geography teacher couldn't find a map, and the math teachers had no chalk. And no one knew where the principal was.

Mrs. Wilburham, the school secretary, was going batty. People were calling her on the brand-new, high-tech, state-of-the-art intercom system, but darn if she could figure out how to answer them. She flipped switches all over the fancy console, but the best she could do was connect the kitchen to the teachers' lounge.

The office was getting more and more crowded. Teachers, students — everyone had a problem or a question for her, as if she were the answer lady. She didn't even know how to work this new-fangled telephone, with its million buttons and lights. If she did, she'd be calling the police right now to report a missing principal.

First period was nearly over, the German teacher was trying to figure out the intercom, the nurse was studying the telephone, and the entire history department was at the counter asking for books — when in strolled the principal himself, along with a boy and girl. And taking their sweet old time about it, too: laughing, jabbering, couldn't care less that the school was falling down around the secretary's ears.

"You're late," said Mrs. Wilburham, not even trying to disguise her displeasure.

The principal pretended to be shocked. "We *are?*" He looked down at his accomplices. "Well," he shrugged, "I guess we'll all have to go to Late Room."

The three of them broke up laughing. He then looked up the kids' schedules, scribbled out a late note for each, and sent them on their way — but not before shaking hands with them and saying with a wink, "See you at lunch."

Mrs. Wilburham bit her tongue. She had trained five principals in her lifetime. Apparently this one was going to take some doing.

She had to admit, though, once he decided to show up, things did get done. Within five minutes, the gym people got their footballs, the geography teacher her map, the mathematicians their chalk, the history department its books. He showed her how to get an outside line on the telephone, and he played the intercom console like Liberace at the piano.

There were only five minutes left of first period when he flipped the toggle labeled ALL RE-CEIVERS and made his opening remarks to the school:

"Good morning, everyone.

"I apologize to you all for not speaking to you during homeroom. I had some pressing business elsewhere.

"Let me make it plain that this is not my official greeting. That will come in a couple of weeks, when we have our opening assembly in the new auditorium. That's when all of us will meet all of

19

you and when we will learn the identity of our school mascot, the selection of which you will be involved in.

"In the meantime, let's you and I and Plumstead get to know each other. Over the last couple of years, we've all felt a little like orphans now and then, haven't we? Not enough seats. Not enough classrooms. Shifting school boundaries. We were never really sure where we belonged, were we?

"Well, I'm here to tell you that's all over. I'm here to tell you now we have our own place, our own house. I'm here to say . . . welcome home."

The principal flipped the toggle off, laid down the mike, and went into his office.

Someone was there.

5

The boy had his back to the door, but Mr. Brimlow knew at once who it was. The green sneakers, the pickle-shaped skateboard . . . it could only be . . . "Dennis Johnson, I presume?"

The boy turned, smiled. "You can call me Pickles."

The principal smiled back. "I'll work on it."

They shook hands.

Mr. Brimlow did not need a school record to inform himself about this student. For the past several years, Pickles Johnson had been perhaps the most famous grade-schooler in Cedar Grove.

Pickles Johnson was an inventor. He invented everything from gadgets to excuses.

One day in Second Avenue Elementary, for example, Pickles had a problem. It was the day of the weekly spelling test, and he hadn't studied for it. He had to get out of taking it.

As the test was about to begin, the teacher noticed Pickles madly scratching his chest. When she unbuttoned his shirt, she saw a hundred little red spots and heard Pickles groan, "Chicken pox." She sent him to the nurse.

Five minutes later he was back, escorted by the nurse, who handed the teacher the cause of the "chicken pox": a red felt-tip marker.

For punishment, Pickles had to stay after school and write "I will not lie to my teacher" one hundred times on the blackboard. Only then could he go home.

The teacher left the room for no more than five minutes. When she returned, to her utter amazement, the sentences were on the board. Pickles was gone.

The teacher did not suspect that she had fallen victim to one of Pickles' first inventions: the chalk glove. It was a contraption made of clothes-hanger wire. It had ten "fingers," each one of which held a piece of chalk. Placing all ten fingers against the blackboard at once gave Pickles the ability to write ten letters — ten words — ten sentences at the same time. By actual count, he had written 120 sentences before taking off.

The next day he proudly showed his invention to the teacher, who was too amused and impressed to punish him further.

Pickles' most famous inventive moment, and the one which earned him his nickname, happened over Christmastime when he was seven. From the moment his mother and father brought home the Christmas tree, little Dennis wanted to decorate it. He kept begging, "Let's do it now!" But Mr. and Mrs. Johnson always did the trimming on Christmas Eve, which was still two days away. And they wouldn't even tell him where they kept the balls and tinsel.

So little Dennis took matters into his own hands. The next time Mr. and Mrs. Johnson came into their living room, they found the tree had been trimmed — with pickles. Dill pickles, to be exact, from the jar in the refrigerator. They hung from the tree limbs on hooks made of paper clips.

Mr. Johnson knew history when he saw it. He called a friend who took pictures for the Cedar Grove newspaper. By the time the photographer arrived, Mr. and Mrs. Johnson were practically as green as the tree from inhaling the mixture of pickle and pine fumes. The photographer snapped the picture and said, "I think your son just made himself a new nickname."

Now, as this same Pickles Johnson stood before him, Mr. Brimlow already suspected he was going to like this kid. Unlike most kids, this one looked him right in the eye.

"Well," said the principal, "were you ordered to my office, or did you just decide to pay me a visit?"

"I was ordered," said Pickles.

The principal pointed to the pickle-shaped skateboard. "Would your problem happen to have anything to do with that?"

"My teacher said I have to keep it in my locker," said Pickles, "but it won't fit in my locker."

Mr. Brimlow reached out. "Let's see."

Pickles handed it over. It was quite a piece of work. A casing had been carved from wood, much like a miniature canoe, painted green, and fixed to the sole of the original board.

"Got a name for it?" said the principal.

"Pickleboard."

The principal placed the board on the floor. He rolled it back and forth with one foot. "Smooth," he said. "Good wheels."

Pickles nodded. "The best."

The principal had seen the boy tooling around town on this green footmobile. He had to admit, it *did* look like fun. He pushed off and let it carry him slowly across the office, stopping with a mild bump at the bookcase.

"Always wondered what it was like," he said.

"It's the best fun," said Pickles. "But you have to give it a longer ride than that to *really* tell."

Their eyes locked. They were both thinking the same word: *hallway*.

"Your teacher's right," said the principal. "School is no place for this thing."

"What could happen?" said Pickles.

"What could *happen*?" echoed the principal as

he wobbled through the doorway and into the outer office, where he collided gently with the back of Mrs. Wilburham's swivel chair.

Mrs. Wilburham pitched forward. "What in the name of — ?" She looked up in time to see her boss set a course for the doorway, sail out into the hall, and bump into the far wall.

Pickles followed. "When you really get going," he said, "it's like you're flying." He looked down the long length of the hallway, at the shiny, newly waxed linoleum. "Especially on a new floor like this."

The principal pushed off — one push, two, three — picked up his push foot, wobbled, wobbled, pushed again, climbed on, and went sailing past the startled nurse who was stepping out of the infirmary. Past the library he sailed, faster and faster, the wheels humming like a blender on puree.

Behind him, running now, the boy yelled, "Yahoo!" Ahead of Mr. Brimlow loomed the end of the hallway, the door to room 101, Mrs. Volker's geography class. "How do I stop this thinnnnnnnnng?!" he yelled just as the bell rang, just as Mrs. Volker opened her door, just as he shot past her nose and into the room, swatting the huge globe of the planet on his way to a crash landing with Mrs. Volker's desk.

In the stunned stillness that followed, the only sound was the whir of the globe, spinning like the earth gone mad. The class, many of them frozen halfway out of their seats, gaped in mute wonderment as their principal rearranged a few things on Mrs. Volker's desk, stood tall, straightened his bow tie, cleared his throat, pointed out the door and down the hallway with the pickle-shaped skateboard, and bellowed sternly: *"That's* what could happen!"

Moments later, in the crowded hallway, Mr. Brimlow whispered to Pickles, "That was *some* ride." Then he told Pickles he would not be allowed to bring the board to school anymore. He could pick it up in the main office on his way home.

And then he invited him to lunch.

6

Back in his office, Mr. Brimlow took off his jacket. What a morning! Many times he had imagined his first day as principal, but never did he picture himself getting hijacked in a yellow bus and then hoofing it back to school with a pair of sixth-graders.

It was the best beginning he could have had. Not only was he not going to fire the portly, hairy-eared bus driver, he intended to thank him. He had gotten to know Salem Brownmiller and Eddie Mott better than he would have in three years from behind his desk. In fact, walking and talking with them, he had been struck with the inspiration to invite them to lunch. Then the Johnson boy. Yes, indeed, he was already getting a Plumstead family feeling.

He now turned his attention to a little matter that had been nagging him all morning: the sour-pussed girl, "Butthead."

Starting with the A's, he went through the

sixth-grade records, looking for that face, trying to imagine it with a smile. It didn't show up until the W's, and even then the smile was pretty skimpy. Her last name was Wyler, her first name was Elizabeth. And her middle name — surprise, surprise — was Sunshine.

Sunny Wyler was on her way. She was sure she would be the first kid ever transferred out of poopy Plumstead. In first period math, the teacher had made them write out all twelve times tables. She made sure she got every one wrong. For example, she wrote 2 x 2 = 94. And 5 x 5 = 1. And 7 x 3 = 23,962.

And that wasn't all. She did them in her super-subminiature writing. This was one of Sunny's great talents. She could make numbers and letters so small that at first glance they all looked like dots. Most grown-ups found them impossible to read. Wee writing, she called it, and it was perfect for secret notes to her best friend Hillary. And maybe also for getting herself kicked out of here and transferred to Hillary's school, Cedar Grove.

She had squeezed the entire set of tables — one hundred and forty-four multiplications — into the lower right-hand corner of the paper in a space about the size of two postage stamps. Of course, a pointy pencil was essential to wee writing, so she made a further nuisance of herself by going to the pencil sharpener exactly nineteen times.

And now she sat in second-period English. The teacher, Ms. Comstock, had given them an in-class writing assignment: "My Most Interesting Day Last Summer."

Sunny wrote:

> *my most interesting day last summer happened on the 4th of july. my little brother was liting a cherry bomb and it went off and blue his noze off. he was groping around for it but he couldnt find it becauz it flu in thru the kitchen window and into a bowl of serial that my father was eeting. only he wasnt looking. then he took a spoon full of serial and screemed. a noze!! i just bit into a noze!!!! yuck!!!!!!!!!!! and the am-bulince came and took my brother to the hospittle and they took the noze along in a plastic bag fool of ice kubes so it wouldnt rot and they sood his noze back on. but the problem was when my brother cam outside it was raining reely hard and he drounded becauz they sood his noze on upside down!!! yes it sure was the most interesting day around here in a long time.*

Sunny signed not only her name, but her home address and telephone number as well. She wanted to make sure the school authorities could reach her as soon as they decided to expel her.

When she finished, she looked up and found someone smiling at her. It was the dodo from the bus. What was it with this kid?

He was two seats up in the next row, too far to smack or kick. Then she thought of a trick she often used to get rid of her little brothers when they were bugging her. She stared straight back at the dodo, stuck her finger up her nose, and pretended to pull out a boogie. She rolled the pretend boogie between her thumb and forefinger into a perfect little pretend boogie ball. She sat the pretend boogie ball on her thumb, dug the nail of her middle finger in behind it, and while the dodo's eyes got round as quarters, she fired. The dodo ducked, almost falling out of his seat. Sunny almost forgot herself and laughed.

Shortly before the period ended, Ms. Comstock was called to the classroom door. She came back in holding a small white piece of paper. She looked over the class. "Elizabeth Wyler?" she said.

Sunny raised her hand. Ms. Comstock came down the aisle and gave her the piece of paper. The teacher's face revealed nothing. The bell rang.

Sunny turned in her essay and gathered up her books and joined the mob heading out. She unfolded the piece of paper. She read it:

Elizabeth Wyler —
Please report to the principal's
office at lunchtime.

Already!

Did the math teacher run down to the office with her tiny terrible times tables? Was the brand-new school bugged? Did a hidden camera in the ceiling record her essay as she wrote it, or catch her flipping the pretend boogie ball at the grinning dodo?

The principal's office. She couldn't believe it. Things were going faster and easier than she had even hoped. She could picture herself washing her hair tonight. Heck, before the day was over, she might be sitting alongside Hillary Kain in Cedar Grove Middle School!

7

Eddie Mott left Ms. Comstock's English class in a daze. Shattered were his hopes that his first day of middle school would go smoothly. So far he had been threatened by a grumpy girl, used as a football, hijacked, stranded at a gas station, and targeted by a boogie-shooter, none other than the same grumpy girl. What was the matter with her, anyway? Come to think of it, what was the matter with him? Why did he keep looking and smiling at her?

And this changing class business. Boy, things were sure a lot simpler when you just went to one room in the morning and stayed there all day. Luckily, he hadn't had to find his first class, because that's when he was walking halfway across town with Salem Brownmiller and the principal (the only good part of the day so far, and of course it happened outside of school). For second-period English, the principal himself had given him directions.

The stampeding herd carried him down the hallway. He looked at his schedule. Next was science in room 117. He looked up. He was passing the boys' gym. He had no idea where he was. He needed help.

A boy was bending over a water fountain, taking a drink. Eddie tapped him on the back, "Excuse me."

The boy kept drinking. He tilted his head. One eyeball rolled upward till it was staring at Eddie, while the boy's mouth continued slurping water. Eddie waited.

At last the boy finished and stood. Eddie came up to his shirt pocket. "What?" said the boy.

Eddie gulped. "I — uh — I'm looking for room one-seventeen. Do you think you could show me the way?"

The giant boy blinked a few times, then he smiled. "Sure. You in sixth grade?"

"Yeah," said Eddie. "First day in middle school." He hoped his voice wasn't shaking. Actually, he felt more at ease now that the boy was smiling.

The boy reached for the schedule. "Can I see that?" Eddie handed it over. The boy studied it, nodded. "Yep . . . ol' one-seventeen all right. Okay." He gave the schedule back. He leaned down. He put one hand on Eddie's shoulder and pointed with the other. "You go down these stairs here. When you get to the bottom, you turn —

let's see — right, yeah, and then there's a door, and you go through that, and you're there."

Eddie looked up. He smiled back. "O-*kay*. Thanks a lot."

"No problem," said the boy, his smile really big now. "Good luck, dude."

Eddie sailed through the door and down the stairs. *Dude — wow! An eighth-grader called me dude. They're not so bad after all. All you have to do is be nice to them.*

The bell rang. The other kids were gone. Uh-oh, he must be late! At the bottom of the stairs he turned right and looked for the door. There it was. He opened it . . . and instead of desks and students and a teacher, he saw pipes. Big pipes, little pipes, running up the walls, across the ceiling. And squatting on the floor were two big metal things. Well, it *did* look kind of scientific.

He peered back outside. Another door across the way. He tried it. It was a small room. A long-nosed man was sitting at a desk, drinking from a mug.

Eddie blurted out, "This isn't room one-seventeen, is it?"

The man was rising, saying, "What?" but Eddie already knew the answer. He dashed back to the stairway and up as far as he could go. He pushed through doors and into a long, deserted hallway. A mile of lockers and doorways and silence. His heart thudded against the English book he held

34

to his chest. He had a vision of every classroom and locker door swinging open and faces leaning out of every one and braying: "YOU'RE LATE, SIXTH-GRADER!"

He took only a couple of steps before realizing he could never walk into room 117 this late, even if he ever found it. Somewhere nearby he heard horns and drums . . . then steps, coming from up ahead. Then a voice within: *Hide!*

8

Eddie barged through the nearest door. He found himself in the back of a wide, spacey room, a music room. Up front, kids were honking and thumping and plinking on instruments. There was an open door to his right, against the back wall. He ducked into it.

It was a large closet. It was shadowy, but light from the big room revealed it to be a storage area for musical instruments. Everywhere round brassy mouths gaped fishlike at him, threatening to blare and give him away. He picked his way as carefully as possible through the instruments and cases to the back of the closet. Here, in the corner behind a tuba, it was dark. He sat on the floor, his knees up to his chin.

Twice during the period, someone reached into the closet for an instrument. But no one came for the tuba.

Outside he could hear the instructor saying over and over: "Your lips go like this . . . like this . . .

okay now . . . blow." This would usually be followed by silence, followed by, "no . . . like *this*," followed by what sounded like the squawk of an animal whose tail had been stepped on.

Confusingly, there were other sounds, too, but not like any instrument he had ever heard: twangs, tweets, and bonks. This was *music*?

But all this was background to the feelings churning inside Eddie. There was no use pretending anymore that he wanted to be a grown-up middle-schooler. What he really wanted was to be back at Brockhurst Elementary. He wanted to stay in the same classroom all day. He wanted stars and turkeys on his spelling tests. He wanted to wear his Daffy Duck pin. He wanted recess.

And now, suddenly, he wanted to go to the bathroom. Oh boy! He clenched his teeth. He tried to think about other things, like baseball and raising the flag every morning with Roger Himes. Oh, life used to be so simple. You had to go, you raised your hand, and a minute later: relief. Now, he didn't dare move till the end of the period. It didn't help that against the wall a couple of feet away stood, invitingly, a saxophone.

The bell!

Eddie shot out of the closet, out of the music room, down the hall, around the bend, down the stairs, up the hall, searching for a door that said BOYS. . . .

There!

He burst in. There was a sound, a sound he had heard before, a sound that he himself had sometimes made before:

"hhhh-Thooo!"

Just as he realized it was the sound of a hocker loading and firing, he was hit. Smack in the left ear. He froze.

Someone said, "Hey, that don't count. He got in the way."

Somebody else said, "It counts, man. My turn . . . *hhh-Thooo!*"

A second hocker grazed his chin.

He was caught in the crossfire of a spit fight.

"I got him in the ear, man! That's two points!"

"It's no points! It's only a sixth-grader!"

"Yer cheatin', man!"

"*Yer* cheatin'!"

"Yeah?"

"Yeah!"

"*hhh* — "

"*hhhh* — "

"THOOO!"

"THOOO!"

Eddie bolted for the nearest stall and locked himself in. There was no longer any question of going to the bathroom. His bladder had turned to ice. His only concern now was walking out of here alive.

He pulled off some toilet paper and mopped out his left ear. He wished he knew more about the human ear. He knew there was an eardrum in there somewhere. He had always pictured it as a tiny bongo drum. Would it halt the seepage? Or would the hocker ooze on through, deeper and deeper into the dark catacombs of his ear? Would he lose his hearing? Horrible scenes came to him, pictures of people at supermarket checkout lines, gawking in wonder and disgust at the fat-lettered headlines in the *Star* and *Midnight*:

> ## BOY'S BRAIN
> ## TURNS TO
> ## MUSH!
>
> ## HOCKER BLAMED!
>
> ## EIGHTH-GRADERS
> ## SOUGHT IN
> ## BATHROOM MURDER!

Frantically, he cocked his head and thumped the side of it, trying to jettison the runaway ooze. As he did so, there came a rattle and a bumping upon the door of his stall. He looked down, into a grinning, upside-down face occupying the space between the bottom of the stall door and the floor. "Hi, there," said the grinning face. Eddie looked up and saw the toe ends of a pair of sneakers hanging over the top of the door. One of the spitters was hanging upside down on his stall door.

He heard the telltale intake of breath, the loading: "Hhhh — " He glanced down. The mouth was no longer grinning. It was puckered. It occurred to him how much a mouth about to hockerate resembles a mouth about to kiss, but he felt certain he was not about to be kissed.

"THOOO!"

Eddie's English book flew to his face, just in time to catch the missile. The bell for next period rang. The face and feet disappeared. A moose call, a Tarzan yell, a gush of hallway noise as the door opened, and then silence. Merciful silence.

Eddie tore off some more toilet paper and wiped off the intercepted hocker. He was beginning to wonder if he had made some kind of terrible mistake. Maybe he had gotten on the wrong bus that morning. (Served him right, telling his mom to stay home.) Maybe he had boarded the bus to Hell. And now he was going to miss yet *another* class.

"Is that you, Eddie?"

He clamped his breath. He froze. Who was speaking?

"Eddie Mott?"

The voice seemed to be coming from another stall. Where had he heard that voice?

"Eddie."

He leaned down till he could see beneath the side panel of his stall. Two stalls up was a face, smiling, upside down, long curly brown hair pooling on the floor.

"Salem *Brownmiller*?"

"In the flesh."

"What — what — ?"

"It's a long story. Let's get out of here first."

Which they did. Fast.

9

In the hallway, Eddie went to the nearest locker and began knocking his forehead into it. "I'm in trouble," he whined. "*Big* trouble."

Salem pulled him away. "You're going to be in bigger trouble if you don't stop that. What's the matter?"

"What's the *matter*? Every time I look around, I'm in an empty hallway. I missed two classes so far, and the only one I went to, somebody flicked a boogie at me. And now I'm missing *another* class. I'm lost. I don't know where I am. I wanna go home."

"Whoa!" said Salem, whipping out her notepad and pen. "What was that about a boogie?"

Eddie just stared at her — a glazed, vacant look if she ever saw one. If he was going to do her any good, she was going to have to nurse him along. Hurriedly she jotted in her notepad:

flicked boogie
glazed, vacant look

Then she spoke gently to him. "It's okay, Eddie. First-day jitters, that's all. Let me see your schedule."

He handed it over.

"Hey, same as me! Art in one-oh-three."

"I don't know where it is."

Salem returned his schedule. "We'll find it together." She took his arm. "Come on."

They walked.

"Okay," said Salem, "go ahead, ask me."

"Ask you what?"

"What was I doing in the boys' room?"

"I don't care. I just want to be in class. *Any* class."

"Okay, I'll tell you anyway." She pushed a door open. "Down these stairs. But first you want to know *how* I did it, right? So say how."

"How?"

Salem pushed open the door at the bottom of the stairs. They were in another deserted hallway. Salem reached into her book bag and with a flourish drew out a long, black, silky scarf. "*This*" — she bunched up her hair and wrapped the scarf about her head, like a turban — "is how."

Eddie cooperated just enough to grant her a grudging glance. Sure enough, she could have passed for a boy.

"It's my writer's scarf," she said, unwrapping and returning it to the book bag. "I always wear it when I'm writing. But sometimes it comes in handy for other things, too. At first I was going to get a white one, but then I thought, Nah, that's too common, just what you'd expect a girl to pick. So I got black. Mysterious, huh?"

No response from Eddie, who plodded straight ahead while Salem bounced sideways down the hall beside him, jabbering.

"So, now you want to know *why* I did it, right? Well, in a word: research. I've decided to write my story about a boy's first day in middle school instead of a girl's. So I asked myself: Where do you go to find out about boys? Answer: a boys' room, of course. I had study hall last period, so — presto! — there I was." She waved her notepad. "Taking notes. I'll tell ya, you boys are *something*." She said this with a sly grin and a nudge to Eddie's arm, trying to get a rise out of him, but he just plodded on, vacant, glazed. One thing she had decided not to tell him was that she had chosen him to be the model for the boy in the story. From the moment she had seen him sitting in the back of the bus, she knew he had to be her main character.

"So," she said, "what's it like to be a boy?"

No answer. And no wonder. Too general a question. Make it more specific. "So, what's it like to get spit on?"

He wasn't listening. He was glancing about at the room numbers. "Where's one-oh-three?" he demanded.

"Oh, it's down that way," she pointed. "We passed it a couple times, but we were having such a good dialog — "

"No! . . . No!" he screeched and once again began butting a locker.

This is wild, thought Salem. Now he's in an uncontrolled rage. Maybe he's got a multiple personality. That was every writer's dream, to know such a person. She remembered reading about a lady in Minnesota who had seventeen different personalities inside the same body. So far, she had counted two in Eddie Mott:

1. *Glazed, vacant*
2. *Uncontrolled rage*

She wondered if there were more. She wondered if she could bring them out. What a story! But for now, she pulled him away from the locker and tried to calm him down. It was then that they heard a yell from up the hall: "Stop that hamster!"

A small brown furry bundle was racing down the hallway at them. Around a corner several kids came careening, sneakers squealing like Michelins on the brand-new floor. "Stop it!"

Eddie just stood there, half expecting the furball to leap up and rip his throat out; it was about the only thing that hadn't happened to him. Meanwhile, Salem quickly dropped her book bag to the floor, set it on its side, and held it open, right in the path of the oncoming animal. The harboring darkness, the crannies formed by the papers and books within — it was too inviting for the hamster to resist. Into the green tunnel it scooted, into the back and bottom of the dark.

Salem lifted the book bag and slung it over her shoulder. The pursuers, three of them, came sneaker-squealing to a halt. "He in there?" the tallest one asked, catching his breath.

"He is," replied Salem.

"Well, fork 'im over. He's ours."

Salem's eyebrows arched. "How do *I* know that?"

The boy snarled, "Because I said so."

Eddie edged behind Salem.

Salem sniffed, "That isn't a reason."

The boy looked at his sidekicks, back to Salem. "We found it outside. It's ours." He put his hand out. He snarled, "Here."

Salem snarled back, "I wouldn't give *yyyew* a carbuncle off my nose, if I *had* a carbuncle."

The tall boy's face got downright ugly. He thrust his hand in front of Salem's face. "Girl, the hamster. *Now*."

Salem embraced her book bag with both arms. She tried to make the same gargly sound that the spitters in the boys' room had made. "*hhhh* . . . one more inch, and I'll spit in your face." She pulled Eddie up to her, she put her arm around him. "And so will he."

46

The next movement came from up the hall —
a door opening, a teacher calling: "Hey, there, get
where you're going. No loitering."

Salem and Eddie started walking. The boys,
clearly eighth-graders, started walking, right behind them, inches behind them. Down to the end
of the hallway, turn left, down another hall. Even-
tually art 103 loomed ahead, and so did the question: Which was better, walk into class with half
the period over, or continue this nerve-wracking
parade?

Salem thought about it. Eddie didn't think. Eddie couldn't think. It was all he could do to remain
conscious. All he knew was that a pack of scowling
eighth-graders was following him down a deserted
hallway, and that they had been told that he would
spit in their faces. He was sure that if it were not
for Salem wrapping her arm around his and pulling him along, he'd be lying back up the hallway
by now, the eighth-graders finishing him off, a
carcass, buzzard meat.

And then they were veering into . . . a familiar
place . . . the office, where they had been this
morning. There was the secretary, and there went
the eighth-graders right on down the hallway.
And there was the principal, Mr. Brimlow, coming
out of his office with a big, surprised smile, saying,
"Well, well, look who's early for lunch!"

10

Mr. Brimlow was delighted that two of his lunch guests had showed up early. Especially Salem Brownmiller, who seemed to know what was required better than he, so he simply put her in charge, and soon both he and Eddie Mott were following her orders — dragging in a table from the guidance counselor's office, running to the cafeteria for napkins and utensils and such.

It was in the cafeteria that Miss Brownmiller looked up at him and said, "It *is* going to be catered, isn't it?"

The principal stared at her. "Catered?"

"Yes, from here. Somebody will bring our meals to your office on a big tray, or maybe a cart with wheels, with silver lids over our meals to keep them warm — " She stopped; with a look of rising horror she studied the blank expression on his face. "Mister *Brimlow*, we weren't going to brown *bag* it, were we?"

Mr. Brimlow gulped. "Oh, no . . . of course not."

And so Mr. Brimlow made arrangements with the cafeteria manager to have five hot meals delivered to his office at 11:50 sharp.

The hot entrée for the day, they discovered, was sloppy joe fajitas. "Great!" chimed Salem on the way back to the office. "We'll have a Mexican theme. You should always have a theme for a catered luncheon, don't you think?"

Mr. Brimlow cleared his throat; he nodded, "Oh, yes . . . quite."

As it turned out, there was barely time enough to set the table, much less decorate *à la* Mexico, for lunchtime was upon them.

Eddie Mott could not believe it. The girl standing in the office doorway was Miss Grumpy herself. He had wondered who the other place settings were for, but he couldn't imagine anyone inviting The Grump for lunch.

He watched in amazement as Mr. Brimlow went right up to her all jolly and shook her hand. "Well, hello, Miss Wyler. I see you got my note. Come on in."

The Grump looked confused. She took one step and stopped. She looked at Eddie. She looked at the table. She said, "Aren't I in the wrong place?"

"I don't think so," said the principal. "Where do you think you ought to be?"

She looked straight up at him. "Cedar Grove?"

Now it was the principal who was confused.

"Cedar Grove? Why should you be there?"

"Because of the stuff I did."

Mr. Brimlow studied her. He jiggled one wing of his bow tie. He folded his arms. "I see. Well, what stuff might that be?"

The Grump counted them off on her fingers. "In math class I wrote the times tables so small that the teacher will probably go blind trying to see them all. In English class I wrote something ridiculous about my most interesting day last summer. It was all lies. And" — she pointed to Eddie — "I flicked a boogie ball at that dodo." Everyone froze, as if fearing, waiting for her hand to go to her nose. "*And*," she concluded, "I've had a rotten attitude ever since I got on the bus."

There was silence and stillness, except for the slow nod of Mr. Brimlow's head. At last he said, "I see. Well. What do you think we should do about you?"

The Grump answered at once. "Expel me. I'm a rotten apple. If I hang around much longer, I'll probably infect the whole school."

Eddie glanced over at Salem. She was writing furiously in her notepad, the tip of her tongue peeping from the corner of her mouth.

The Grump took another look at the table. The confused expression returned to her face. "I *am* being expelled, aren't I? Isn't that why I'm here?"

Mr. Brimlow gave a small, regretful shrug. "I'm

afraid not, Sunny. The brutal truth is, you've been
invited to have lunch with us."

Sunny, Eddie repeated to himself. *Sunny?*

And then Mr. Brimlow was bringing her over.
"Sunny Wyler . . . this dodo also goes by the name
of Eddie Mott." Shaking hands with her, trying
to avoid her vicious scowl. "Sunny Wyler . . .
Salem Brownmiller." Salem's eyes lighting up, as
if she had just opened a great birthday present,
pumping the girl's hand: "*Pleased* to meet you,
Sunny."

And then the smell of sloppy joes filled the
room. In rolled a double-decker cart pushed by a
white-aproned cafeteria lady.

"*Olé!*" piped Salem.

Mr. Brimlow clapped his hands. "All *right*! Time
to eat. Let's sit down, gang."

Salem, Sunny, and Eddie took their places. Mr.
Brimlow started to help the cafeteria lady, but
she waved him away. "Oh, no, Mister Principal.
You sit." She was crisp and efficient and dignified,
she wore her hair in a bun with a butterfly bar-
rette, and she obviously knew her stuff. Perhaps
she had once worked in a major hotel or a mil-
lionaire's mansion. Mr. Brimlow sat.

The cafeteria lady distributed plates. "Will
there be another?" she asked, noting the empty
place setting.

"We hope so," said the principal.

She laid down a fifth plate. Then came the food. From the upper rack of the cart she took three large, covered bowls and placed them on the table. With a flourish not unlike that of a matador, she removed the lids to reveal: a tossed salad . . . a steaming vat of sloppy joe . . . and a tall stack of tortillas.

"*Olé!*" said Salem.

"*Sí, sí!*" said Mr. Brimlow.

Sunny said nothing, though her head swiveled slowly toward the other girl.

The cafeteria lady then provided each place with a half pint of milk and two plastic-wrapped chocolate chip cookies. She stepped back to consider her work. Her finger went up. "Ah — straws." She plunged her hand into the deep pocket of the apron, almost to the elbow — her hand shot back up with such force and speed that it smacked her in the chin; her eyes were suddenly big as tortillas.

As the principal and three students watched in wonder, the apron pocket began to move — to the left, to the right, a rumpled, dumpled, bulgy ball of movement — and then the dignified cafeteria lady was tearing off her apron and flinging it into the air. The apron landed on the tortilla stack and went swooping about the table, knocking plastic forks and plates until it draped itself over the salad bowl and at last was still. And now a faint rustling could be heard beneath the ghostly apron, and another, tinier sound, like chewing.

"Don't worry," Salem told the others, "it's only a hamster." She pulled the apron away —

"It *is* a hamster!" exclaimed the principal, as the dignified lady fled.

Salem reached for it, the principal reached for it, and the hamster took the only escape route available, which happened to be into — and out of — the sloppy joe bowl. It leaped upon Sunny's shirt and onto the floor. Dripping orange and shedding hamburger bits, it dashed in frantic patterns about the office while Brimlow, Brownmiller, and Mott gave chase.

"The door!" cried the principal, but not soon enough, for the sloppy joed rodent already had a nose in the outer office, and then — miraculously — it was in the air, snatched by a hand that appeared as if from nowhere. And then the rest of the body appeared — a boy with green sneakers.

Mr. Brimlow hurried to him. "Welcome, and great catch there!" He pumped the boy's free hand and turned to the rest of them. "Friends, may I present our other guest for lunch today, Mr. Dennis Johnson."

11

Within five minutes the squirming hamster was cleaned up and deposited in an unused fish tank borrowed from the science lab.

At that point Sunny Wyler nodded to the sloppy joe bowl and announced, "I am not eating anything a hamster crawled through."

"What?" said Mr. Brimlow, looking shocked. "That gives it flavoring."

Sunny just stared at the principal until he laughed. He reached out and tweaked her nose. "Just kidding." He wondered how long it would take before he saw a smile on this kid's face.

Another five minutes passed as Mr. Brimlow called the kitchen and had a new batch of sloppy joe and tortillas delivered, forget the salad. This time the food was brought in by a man. He said the dignified lady had come back trembling and had told the manager she was returning to her old job at a private boarding school. The straws were still in the pocket of her abandoned apron. The man took them out, tossed them onto the table, and left.

"I'm not using any straw that some animal's lips were on," declared Sunny Wyler.

"Fine," said the principal, "you have my permission to drink straight from the carton." He was beginning to think she was serious about being expelled from school.

For some time after Mr. Brimlow said, "Dig in," no one spoke. He decided to break the ice himself with a question to the Johnson boy. "So, Dennis, considering your nickname, you must be pretty fond of pickles, huh?"

Pickles had not folded his sloppy joe filling into a tortilla, Mexican style, as had the others. He had instead laid a tortilla flat on his plate and spread a layer of sloppy joe over it, creating a sort of small pizza. He cut the pie into neat, equal-sized wedges.

"I hate pickles," he said.

"Really?"

"Yeah. I think they're neat-looking, and I like how the name sounds, but I can't stand the taste. My mother was always giving me one with my sandwich. That's why I put them on the Christmas tree, to get rid of them."

Mr. Brimlow filled in the other kids on how Pickles got his name.

Salem snickered. "Good thing you didn't decide to hate bananas."

"Bananas Johnson," giggled Eddie.

Trying to include Sunny Wyler, Mr. Brimlow said, "What food would you hang on a Christmas tree, Miss Wyler, if you had to?"

"Monkey brains," said Sunny Wyler. While the rest of the kids laughed, her sneer made it clear what she thought of this silly conversation.

Salem Brownmiller was jotting again in her notepad.

"Now, Miss Brownmiller," said the principal, "there must be a story behind your name as well. Don't tell me you're a witch."

Salem laid her pencil down. "That's not far off, actually. My mother and father met each other in Salem, Massachusetts. My father says she bewitched him. He said he wanted his firstborn to be named Salem, whether it was a boy or girl. I happen to think it's better as a girl's name, but of course I'm prejudiced. Actually, I didn't like my name at first; that is, when I got old enough to realize I *had* a name, of course. I loathed it. But then when I decided to be a writer, I started liking it, and now I *love* it. I mean, if you're a writer you need a name that people will remember when they see it with all those other names on the bookshelves, right? As for my last name, I don't know, I'm still debating whether to change it or not. I mean, Brown? Miller? *Together?* How common can you get! Sometimes I have nightmares about marrying somebody named Jones and hyphenating my name. Can you see it? Salem Brownmiller-Jones? Egad!"

"Egad, indeed," echoed Mr. Brimlow quickly, seizing the chance to silence Miss Brownmiller lest she talk the entire lunch period away. "And now Miss Wyler — " All heads turned toward the sour-faced girl with the DEATH TO MUSH-ROOMS T-shirt, now also featuring a tiny orange paw print from her brief encounter with the hamster. "Salem loves her name. How do you feel about yours?"

"I think it's dumb," she said.

"Is there a story behind it?"

"No."

"Well," the principal smiled, "it didn't fall down out of the sky and land on your birth certificate, did it?"

Salem and Eddie Mott snickered; Sunny glared. Mr. Brimlow decided not to be so flip with Wyler.

"It's not a *story*," Sunny snipped.

All were silent.

She waved her fajita. "It's just dumb. When I was born, my mother said it was like a little ray of sunshine."

Before Eddie Mott realized what was happening, the words were out of his mouth: "So what did she name you? Little Ray?"

This time it wasn't snickers, it was outright

laughter. Salem thumbed back to a previous page in her notepad entitled *Mott Personalities* and wrote:

3. Comedian

"Yeah?" Sunny snarled. "Well, the joke was on her, 'cause I'm a black cloud everywhere I go. If you let me hang around long enough, pretty soon everybody'll be going off to the shrink, they'll be so depressed." She ripped a bite from her fajita. She looked up at the faces around the table; she settled on Mr. Brimlow's. "See? Already I'm ruinin your lunch."

Brimlow chomped on his fajita. "Not ruining *my* lunch." He polled the others. "Is Sunny ruining anybody's lunch here?"

Everyone shook their heads no, Eddie Mott a trifle belatedly.

"Mister Mott — " said the principal, and almost regretted it when he saw the boy tense up.

"Eddie, you and I seem to be the only ones here today without unusual names. I'll tell you, I almost feel positively boring."

Salem spoke, with a kindly glance toward Eddie. "You don't need an interesting name to be an interesting person."

Mr. Brimlow nodded. He smiled. "You're absolutely right, Brownmiller. Let that be the amen for this little discussion."

A warm tide rose in Mr. Brimlow's breast. He really liked these kids. He wanted more of them. "Mister Mott," he said, "as I recall from your record, you were a flag-raiser at Brockhurst. How would you like the same job here at Plumstead?"

The boy's expression barely changed, but for a moment that lost look was gone. "Okay," he said with a slight shrug, and Mr. Brimlow knew it was more than just okay.

"And you'll need help, right?" said the principal.

Eddie nodded. "You should always have two people, one to hold the flag and attach it and the other to pull the rope. Sometimes when my partner was absent, I did it all by myself, but it's pretty tricky. You have to be careful never to let it touch the ground."

"Right," agreed Mr. Brimlow. "Well, how about if you work with Johnson here. You can teach him the ropes. You'll both need to be here as soon as the doors open, first bell, every day. Dennis?"

Pickles nodded. "No problem."

Eddie wasn't sure how he felt about this. On the one hand, it was exciting to be paired with a famous person. On the other hand, it was a little scary, too. Eddie couldn't imagine himself telling the great Pickles Johnson what to do. Suppose he got nervous and forgot something? Suppose Pickles wanted to raise a pickle instead of the flag?

Mr. Brimlow got up and walked to the file cabinet, on top of which sat the glass tank with the hamster. "Does anybody know where this critter came from or who it belongs to?"

Salem raised her hand, and against his better judgment he let her speak. She told about the eighth-graders chasing it in the hallway, and how she lured it into her book bag because, "as a writer, one of your most important skills is to put yourself in other peoples' places, so you can understand them and therefore write better about them, which is precisely what I did in this case, except it was a hamster and not a person, of course. I asked myself, Now, if I were a hamster being chased down a hallway, remembering that a hamster is a rodent, what — "

"Okay, Salem" — Mr. Brimlow jumped in — "got the picture. Now, here's what I'm going to do. I'll make announcements, today, tomorrow. If nobody comes forward to claim the critter, well" — he smacked the cabinet — "then we'll keep it right here. Miss Wyler?" The girl looked up. "How would you like to be keeper of the critter?"

She crinkled her face. "Do I have to?"

Mr. Brimlow smiled. "Yes. Be here after school tomorrow."

The bell rang. They were getting up. He held out his hands. Ideas were rushing. "Hold it a second, gang. Thirty seconds, tops. You won't be late. Two quick things. On September eighteenth for the opening assembly we're going to present

Plumstead's new mascot. The students will vote for it. Three choices, one from each grade. I want you guys to come up with the nomination from sixth grade. You'll be a committee of four. Salem, you've just volunteered to be chairman — excuse me, chairwoman."

Outside, the hallway was bustling.

"And let's do this again next week, Wednesday, right here, lunch. Got it? Okay, outta here!"

12

"**I** *hate* it!" grumbled Sunny. "Even worse than I thought I would."

"My school's okay, I guess," said Hillary. "But it would be a lot better with you there."

The two best friends were in Sunny's room after dinner.

"I messed up every chance I got," Sunny went on. "Math class, English. Then I got a note, 'Report to the principal's office.' "

"Wow!" went Hillary.

"Yeah, wow is what I figured. I'm history, right? Expelled. Sayanara, Dumbstead — Cedar Grove, here I come."

"Yeah . . . so?" gasped Hillary. She was chewing on the ear of her teddy bear. Hillary slept over so often that the teddy bear had become a permanent resident of Sunny's bedroom.

"So, you know what it was?"

"What?"

"Lunch."

"*Lunch?*"

"Yeah. I was invited to *lunch* with the principal."

"The *principal?*"

"Yeah. In his office. He's as dorky as the school. He wears a bow tie."

Hillary switched to the bear's other ear. "So why'd he invite you? He friends with your parents or something?"

"Not that I know of. I don't know why. He knew my name. He knew my real middle name."

"Sunshine?"

"Yeah, you believe it?"

"He must have looked you up."

"Yeah, but why? Why me?"

They thought about it, but no answer came.

"And that's not all," said Sunny. "There were three others at the lunch, too."

"Kids?"

"Yeah, three dipsticks — oh — and you know who one was?"

"Who?"

"That Pickles kid."

"Pickles *Johnson*? The one with the skateboard?"

"Yeah. He brought it to school, and the gumball principal gets on it and goes down the hall and crashes into a classroom."

Hillary was goggle-eyed. "You're kidding."

"No. It's all over school."

Hillary edged closer. "Is Pickles cute?"

"*Cute?*" snorted Sunny. "Is *any* boy cute? Besides, he wears green sneakers, like he painted them or something, even on the rubber part, so how cute could he be? He's a meat loaf."

"I hear he does some crazy things," said Hillary. "Did he do anything at lunch?"

Sunny shrugged. "He caught an animal, is about it."

"*What?*"

Sunny told Hillary about the hamster's escapades and capture. "And you want to know the worst of it all? I got the job of taking care of the thing."

Hillary shook her head. "I don't know, your school sounds pretty exciting compared to mine. Maybe I should be getting myself transferred to Plumstead."

"Yeah, right, and have rodents running through your lunch."

The phone rang in the hallway. Sunny raced for it. She returned muttering about dingbats and dipsticks.

"Who was it?" said Hillary.

"Some girl named Salem. You believe that name? She was at the lunch, too. Really weird. The principal made her chairwoman of this committee we're supposed to have to pick the mascot for the school. She wants to have a meeting at her house on Saturday, so we can all get to *know* each other better and get the creative *juices* going. You believe it? She thinks she's thirty-eight years old."

"So," said Hillary. "are you going?"

Sunny sneered. "No way. I told her I will, but I won't. She can get to know the dodo better."

"What dodo?"

"Some little jerk that keeps talking to me and looking and grinning. He thinks I flicked a real snotball at him. What a moron."

Hillary hugged her bear. "Sunny — maybe he likes you!"

Sunny snorted. "Yeah? Well, he can like *this*." She flipped off her shoes and held her feet in Hillary's face. Hillary recoiled. "See these socks? I'm gonna wear them every day till they transfer me, just like the shirt."

"I don't believe I let you talk me into not washing my hair till you're transferred," said Hillary.

Sunny clapped. "We'll reek together!"

"They can use our hair to grease cars!"

The girls knelt face to face, mussing each other's hair.

"We can grow vegetables up there!"

"Cooties!"

"A cootie farm!"

"Eewwww!"

When first bell rang next morning, Eddie Mott went straight to the office and picked up the flag. Back outside, he found Pickles waiting at the pole.

Pickles was holding a brown paper bag. Uh-oh, thought Eddie, what could that be? Some new invention? A funny flag? He hoped Pickles wasn't going to mess things up. To Eddie, raising the flag was a serious, patriotic business.

"Okay," said Pickles, "what do we do?"

Eddie held out the flag. "Take this." Pickles put down the paper bag and took the flag. "Watch me," said Eddie, surprising himself that he had the nerve to give somebody an order.

Eddie unwound the rope from the two-pronged cleat on the pole. He fixed the rope to the two corner holes of the flag. "Okay," he said, "I'm gonna pull it up now. Just let it come out of your hands. Whatever you do, don't let it touch the ground."

Pickles nodded. "Take 'er away."

Eddie began to pull, slowly, as he was taught. When the trailing red-and-white-striped edge of the flag lifted clear of Pickles' hands, Eddie saw him reach down for the paper bag. Well-trained flag-raiser that he was, Eddie kept his eyes respectfully on Old Glory as she rose, but he begged Pickles in silence: *Please, don't mess up*. He heard the bag rustle, and then he heard — could it be? — the notes of reveille: the wake-up song he recognized from army movies.

Keeping his face to the sky, Eddie dragged his eyeballs downward. Pickles was playing a bugle — an old, dented, tarnished horn. Pickles was

66

at attention, facing the school, his cheeks puffed and round as baseballs.

Eddie looked back to Old Glory, heading for the pole top. He got the chills. Patriotism surged through him.

The flag was at the top. Reveille ended. Eddie tied the rope to the cleat. He felt relieved, he felt good. Pickles hadn't messed up, he had made it better. Eddie was on the verge of telling him so when someone burst from the school and headed toward them.

The man was running, waddling actually. He was sort of old and very short, though it was hard to tell how tall he truly was, since he waddled with a stooped-over form. As he got closer, Eddie could see that his eyes were blazing, and then he saw the lips — or more specifically, the lower lip. It was huge. It drooped halfway down his chin, giving the man's face the appearance of a pouting baby. It looked as though his gum had been rolled outward. It looked as though it could be slapped in a roll and mistaken for a short, plump hot dog. And it was shiny, wet and shiny. And it jiggled as the man waddled up to them.

13

The waddling figure was Arnold Wolfgang Hummelsdorf, or — as he was known to generations of Cedar Grove music students — Lips. Lips Hummelsdorf was a lifelong resident of Cedar Grove, and in fact had attended Cedar Grove Junior High before it became a middle school. A look at school photographs from the years 1942 to 1945 would reveal an Arnold Hummelsdorf with a perfectly ordinary-looking mouth.

Neither heredity nor accident of birth was responsible for Hummelsdorf's knockwurst lower lip. Nor was it the woodwinds, and certainly not the percussion. No, it was the brass. Forty years of teaching the trumpet, the trombone, the French horn, and his favorite, the tuba. Forty years of snatching students' instruments and demonstrating. Forty years of kissing mouthpieces that had been spit, sniveled, and slurped into by forty years of coughing, sneezing, wheezing, flu-infested STUDENTS!

Forty years.

Bitter?

Why should he be bitter? Because all he had to show for forty years of teaching musical klunk-heads was a lower lip that hung out like a plum, a salami? Because it presented to the wind a surface as broad as a sail, so that he was in constant danger of getting chapped gums? Because of which he had to continually moisten the lip, making it gleam? Because sometimes students would come up close to him and whip out their combs, believing they could use his lip as a mirror?

No.

The fact is, Hummelsdorf seldom gave his lower lip a thought. To him, it was no different than anyone else's lip.

The source of Hummelsdorf's bitterness could be found five blocks away, in Cedar Grove Senior High School. After many years of glory and prizes and even an appearance in the Orange Bowl Parade, the high school band had fallen on hard times. Last year only fourteen members marched out for the halftimes of football games.

"A disgrace!" blared the newspaper.

"It's embarrassing!" wailed the alumni.

"There's not enough music in the middle school," proclaimed the president of the school board.

And so the blame was dumped on Lips Hummelsdorf. He was called too old, out of step. A young stud music major fresh out of college was brought into Cedar Grove Middle School, and Lips was bumped over to the new place, Plumstead. Not the bargain it appeared to be. Improve the instrumental music program, he was told. Beef up the numbers, he was ordered. They bought new instruments for the college stud and left Lips with the horns and drums he'd been using for half a century.

That is why Lips was waddling out to this young bugler. He hadn't actually heard anything from inside, for his hearing, of all things, was going bad. He simply happened to be looking out a window and saw the boy, ramrod-straight like a private in boot camp, with the bugle to his lips. And now, as he hurried outside, the last few notes lingered in his imperfect ears like the music of the gods.

"You play the trumpet?" he asked the boy, gasping.

"No," the boy answered.

"You play the bugle, you can play the trumpet," Lips said. "Where'd you learn to play?"

The boy shrugged. "Just did."

Hummelsdorf's heart chimed. A born talent. Maybe genius. "You're coming out for band," Lips told him.

"I am?"

"Everybody is coming out for band."

* * *

Eddie thought he was kidding. During second period music, he found out he wasn't.

As Eddie walked into the music room, Hummelsdorf dropped a trombone into his arms. Eddie tried to return it. "I'm sorry, sir, but I don't play this."

"You will," said Lips, pushing it back. "Next."

Eddie took a seat. Salem Brownmiller and Sunny Wyler came in. The teacher gave Salem a drum and Sunny a clarinet. Sunny didn't move. She scowled at the clarinet. She held out the mouth end. The reed was chipped and splintered and pink from lipstick. "I'm not putting my mouth on this," she said, setting the clarinet down. "I'm not playing anything I have to put my mouth on."

"Fine," said Hummelsdorf. He reached into the box by his side. "Here." He handed her a pair of cymbals.

Sunny snatched them and headed for a seat. She was still wearing the DEATH TO MUSHROOMS T-shirt, now with the sloppy joe hamster paw print.

Salem spotted Eddie and took a seat next to him. In amazement they kept their eyes on the front of the room. To the kids now coming into class, Hummelsdorf was handing out kazoos and metal buckets and spoons and empty soda bottles and whistles and washboards. To the last bunch he gave long, thick rubber bands.

Eddie noted that Mr. Hummelsdorf was no

taller standing still than he had been waddling out to the flagpole. His head jutted forward, his back curved, his shoulders drooped, and his potbelly pouted over his belt like a second lower lip. His shape reminded Eddie of . . . "Kidney bean," he whispered to Salem.

Salem frowned in confusion; then she looked at the music teacher, and the frown gave way to a broad grin. "If people were vegetables — "

At that moment a shrieking blast paralyzed the room. Hummelsdorf had put a trumpet to his lips and blown a call to doomsday. Thirty sixth-graders froze in mid-motion, mid-word.

"That's how I bring a class to order," Hummelsdorf told them. "And now I will tell you what we are going to do with the instruments I handed out. As you know, a short time from now we will have our first assembly. Mr. Brimlow, the principal, has asked me to provide music for the occasion. Well, I will provide the music — and *you* will provide the music." He stretched out his arms. "We will *allll* provide the music."

He went on to tell them he was being blamed for the puny size of the high school band, and that he had been ordered to beef up the music program. "Well," he said, "we are going to do better than that. When the curtain opens for the music that day, *every single student* in this school will be onstage. For the first time in history, a whole school will be in the band."

He paused to observe their reaction. Nobody seemed too impressed.

He told them he had composed a special piece of music for the event, and that he would teach every student in Plumstead how to do one or two things on their instrument, no matter what it was.

For the rest of the period, Hummelsdorf went from student to student, demonstrating a twang here, a bang there, a toot, a bonk, a tweet.

With Salem, he showed her how to stutter the stick on the drumskin. "Hold it loose," he told her, "that's the secret. Pretend your wrist is rubber." He showed her: *Brrrrrrr-rrp*. On the third try, she did it.

With Eddie, he ignored the trombone at first and worked on Eddie's face like a sculptor with clay. He molded Eddie's cheeks and shaped his mouth till Eddie was sure he looked like a guppy. Then he put the horn in Eddie's hands and pressed the mouthpiece to his lips and said, "Okay, blow."

Eddie blew. Nothing happened but a faintly metallic gasp.

Hummelsdorf shaped Eddie's lips around the silvery circle of the mouthpiece. "Bring the air up from your feet," he said. "This is not a mouth. It's a nozzle. Squirt the air out. Blast it. Blow!"

Eddie blew. The sound that he heard, and that the rest of the class heard, was the death moo of a constipated cow. But to Hummelsdorf's declining ear, it was a perfectly acceptable note.

"Fine," he said, and moved on.

When he came to Sunny Wyler and told her to beat the cymbals, she replied, "No."

Hummelsdorf blinked. "What?"

"No."

"N-O? *That* no?"

"Right."

Hummelsdorf felt the room fall still and silent about him. He looked her over. She didn't seem to have a physical problem. The T-shirt with DEATH TO MUSHROOMS and a tiny orange paw print was no more ridiculous than most kids' clothes these days. The only really remarkable thing about her was that surly face. It could crack a mirror.

"Why not?" he asked her, holding his temper. "Is it against your beliefs or something?"

The girl stared right back at him. "I don't want to."

This was truly a new one. Not that he had never encountered uncooperative students before, but usually they were sneaky, behind-your-back types. Eyeball lasers from thirty sixth-graders scorched his skin. He could not allow her to win.

"Well," he said, aiming for a tone that was both calm and firm, "unfortunately, it's not up to you, young lady. It's up to me. I have music for the program" — he pointed to a stack of paper on his desk — "and somewhere in there, toward the end, it says 'Cymbals.' Cymbals is you. When we are up on the stage on September eighteenth and I point to you, you will bang the cymbals. Do you understand?"

"No," she said.

"You *will* do it," he said.

"I won't do it," she said.

Amid the barely breathing class they stared at each other. The music teacher changed colors: his neck reddened, his lower lip acquired a bluish tint.

They were like that for perhaps a full minute, then the bell rang. The girl stood. The music teacher jabbed a finger in her face. "You will."

She jabbed a finger at him — "I won't" — and walked out.

14

Salem Brownmiller and Eddie Mott were walking to lunch together.

"Do you *believe* what Sunny did?" said Salem.

Eddie shuddered at the memory. "I thought I was dreaming."

"I think Mr. Hummelsdorf did, too. Did you see, after she did it, he just stood there?"

"Like he was shell-shocked."

"He's probably *still* standing there."

They laughed.

"Want to know something else?" said Salem.

"What?"

"He likes her."

Eddie stopped in his tracks. *"What?"*

"Yeah, I think so." She grabbed his arm and pulled him along.

"How *can* he?" Eddie asked. "After *that*?"

Salem shrugged. "I don't know, I just feel it." She tapped her chest. "Here. I'm practicing listening to my instincts. You don't write just from

76

up here, you know." She patted the top of her head. "See, the best stuff comes from down below, in the subconscious. They don't even look like words, or ideas. I pretend they're little fishes, like with little neon feelers 'cause it's so dark down there. And what I do, see, is *oof!* — "

Salem was so preoccupied that she walked into a teacher standing outside his room. "Excuse me, sir, a thousand pardons," she bowed and backed away and continued on with Eddie. "What I do — this is especially true when I'm writing poetry — I pretend like the top of my brain is a beach, and I'm dropping my fishing line into the water of my subconscious, and if I'm lucky, one of those little fishes will bite, and I pull it up onto the beach. Then it dries out and becomes a word. 'The best words are the bones of visitors from the deep.' Isn't that incredible? I read it in one of my writing books."

You're pretty incredible, too, thought Eddie, who wasn't sure he understood all of that. He said, "I still don't see how Mr. Hummelsdorf can like Sunny."

Salem sang, "Time will tell. And I have another instinct about Sunny and somebody else." They were coming downstairs to the cafeteria hallway. She looked at him. "Want to hear it?"

She said this with a sly grin that warmed Eddie's face and made him afraid to say yes.

As they reached the bottom of the stairs, two

boys who had been standing there turned abruptly and blocked their way. One was skinny, one was fat. Both were nickelheads. Their hair had been cut to less than a half-inch all over, and then nickel-sized circles had been shaved down to the scalp. The result was a polka-dotlike haircut.

The skinny nickelhead pointed to Eddie's brown bag and said, "Lunch tax."

"Huh?" said Eddie.

"Lunch tax. Open your bag."

"Why?" said Eddie. He had thought that after yesterday, he was done with eighth-graders.

"Protection," said the skinny nickelhead. "You pay up, and we see to it that nobody bothers you."

"Right," sneered Salem, who had no bag, "until when?"

The nickelheads grinned at each other. "Till tomorrow."

"Come on, Eddie." Salem pulled him away, but the brown paper bag stayed behind, snatched by the skinny nickelhead, who opened it and began checking out the contents. He pulled out a chocolate pudding cup.

"I'm calling a teacher," said Salem, but before she took a step, the bag was snatched again — this time by Pickles Johnson, who had appeared as if from nowhere.

"You don't want this kid's lunch," Pickles told the stunned nickelheads. "He lives in a pigpen. Rats. Roaches. Garter snakes. I used to deliver papers there. Once a week I had to go inside to collect. I quit my job just so I wouldn't have to. His parents are geeks."

As he spoke he folded the top of the paper bag and handed it back to Eddie. Then, in a blur of handspeed, he snatched the pudding cup from the skinny nickelhead. "You think this is pudding? This isn't pudding. It's probably mashed roaches with bathtub scum. Look — " He tore off the aluminum foil lid, turned the cup upside down, and dumped the contents onto the nickelhead's purple, red-and-white, gold-tongued, transparent bubble-soled, trampoline-treaded sneakers. "Oops," said Pickles. "I guess it *was* pudding."

He dropped the empty cup. Before it landed he was taking off. Before the nickelheads lit out after him, he was up the stairs.

Eddie stared at Salem. "I think my life just got saved."

Principal Brimlow made the intercom announcement once on Thursday, twice on Friday: "We have a lost hamster in the main office. If it belongs to anyone, you may come and claim it."

No one came.

Not even Miss Elizabeth Sunshine Wyler, despite direct orders to report after school.

Teachers were already talking about her. What was her problem? Apparently she knew exactly what she wanted, to get kicked out. Why not give it to her? Punt her over to Cedar Grove, let them deal with her.

Mr. Brimlow brought the hamster tank from his file cabinet to the outer office. The trip sent the animal fleeing to a corner. "I'm taking you home for the weekend, little guy." The hamster stared at him, two black eyes in a ball of caramel-colored fur.

It was nearly five. Everyone else was gone. Two days. Plumstead Middle School was two days old. Someday, with luck, she would be fifty years . old. Someday, these kids would bring *their* kids by and say, "See, that's where I went to school."

Would Wyler be one of them?

He looked at the hamster. He spoke to it. "She will, if I can help it."

He walked down the hallway toward the library.

15

Salem took one step back from the dining room table. She smiled. She nodded. "Perfecto."

It was 1:30 Saturday afternoon. She had told the mascot committee to come at 2:00, but you never knew when people might show up early. Besides, she was simply too excited to let it go until the last minute. Except for the food, the table had been set since ten o'clock.

Salem Brownmiller could no more host an ordinary meeting than Madonna could wear an ordinary outfit. Salem strove, whenever possible, to make every episode of her life an "occasion." Her mother had vetoed use of the elegant lace tablecloth, so she had had to settle for the pale yellow one. Though she was not allowed to use the silverware, she did win her argument to set the table with stainless steel instead of plastic, and with real plates instead of paper.

For the hundredth time she reviewed the sheet

that she had composed and printed out the night
before with her father's desktop publisher:

* MASCOT COMMITTEE MEETING *
Saturday, September 5
2 p.m.

ORDER OF EVENTS
BUFFET
BUSINESS MEETING
("Nominating a mascot
for Plumstead Middle
School")
SOCIAL HOUR
* * *

MUSIC: *Autumn*
by George Winston
* * *

MENU
Potato Chips
Onion Dip
Cold Vegetables (for dipping)
Cheese (cheddar, brie)
Pepperoni Slices
Pickles
Pigs in a Blanket
Grey Poupon
Mints
Periwinkle Punch

Salem had considered phrasing such as "Chips of Potato" and "Dip of Onion," but had rejected them as a little too uppity for this group. And anyway, there was enough elegance in the last item to cover everything.

During the past year Salem had developed the punch herself: a positively exotic blend of five fruit juices, two sodas, and rainbow sherbet. She called it Periwinkle Punch simply because she liked the sound of the two words together. Remembering that made her think of Pickles Johnson at lunch the other day, saying he hated how pickles tasted but liked how they sounded. Apparently he agreed with her that when it came to naming things, whether punch or people, sound could count for more than sense. It was interesting to discover this little tidbit that they had in common.

Salem was even prouder of the punch bowl than the punch. It was colossal, it was crystal, it sparkled like diamonds, it had been in the family for more than a hundred years, and her mother had promised to feed her to the garbage disposal if anything happened to it. The bowl sat regally in the center of the table, no fewer than eighteen matching crystal cups dangling from its rim.

She had chosen the music after trying out a dozen of her parents' tapes. *Autumn* was all piano, pleasant. It would do nicely as background during the buffet and social hour segments.

At precisely 1:45 she poured two large pitchers

of Periwinkle Punch into the crystal bowl. The punch had spent the night in the fridge. She wanted it cold, but not diluted with ice. Then, scoop by scoop, came the rainbow sherbet.

1:50.

Salem paced, sat, looked out the window, looked at the clock, paced, paced . . .

At 2:01 the doorbell rang. She ran, opened the door.

"Eddie! Hi!" She could have hugged him. "Come in."

Eddie came in. They sat in the living room. Salem talked. They waited for the others.

No one came.

By 2:30 Salem was still talking, but her eyes were glistening. "Well," she sighed, "I guess the others couldn't make it. You did tell Pickles, like I asked you, didn't you?"

Eddie stared at her, mouth open. "Uh-oh."

"You forgot."

"Uh-oh."

Salem sighed again. She stood. She inserted the *Autumn* tape. She forced a smile. "Ready to eat?"

"Sure!"

Name tags perched like little white roofs at the four place settings. Salem had tried every possible combination around the table before settling on one. As she had hinted in the hallway the day before, she suspected Eddie had eyes for Sunny.

Though she had since decided not to make him uncomfortable by mentioning it again, she did feel that the least she could do for Eddie was to seat him in the best place relative to Sunny. It boiled down to a question of basic romance: Is it better to seat the girl where the boy can see her best (across the table) or where he can be closest (next to him)? She finally decided on nearness over vision, and placed Sunny's card to Eddie's right.

Of course, none of that mattered now. "There's your name card," she said, pointing, "but you can sit anywhere you like." She poured him some punch and went to the kitchen to microwave the pigs in a blanket.

When she returned, half the potato chips were gone and half the dip.

"Like the dip?" she said.

He nodded with a mouthful and said something that vaguely resembled yes.

"Well," she said, passing the steamy plate of tiny, dough-wrapped hot dogs under his nose, "if you like that, you're gonna *love* these."

Each pig had a toothpick sticking out. It looked like a forest of toothpicks. Eddie chose one. He looked around. "Any mustard?"

Salem set down the plate of pigs. "Right in front of you."

Eddie looked again. "Where?"

Salem pushed a small side dish toward him. "There."

He made a face. "*That's* mustard?"

"The best. It's Grey Poupon."

"Gray — " Eddie went into a sudden spasm. He clamped his hand over his mouth, but not before several bits of potato chip had fired out and sunk into the sherbety foam of his punch. With the mouth cut off, the rest of the spasm exited through Eddie's nose in the form of a rippling, nostril-flapping snort. "Gray" — he croaked — "*poop?*"

Salem rolled her eyes and gave a parental sigh. "No, you goof" — she gave it her best French pronunciation — "Grrrrey Poo-*pawh.*"

She maintained her dignity while the boy suffered through a series of after-snorts. At last he calmed down enough to say, scratchily, "So where's the mustard?"

"It *is* mustard!" The "*is*" came out as a screech.

He held the toothpicked pig shoulder-high, as though the stuff in the side dish might leap for it. "It doesn't *look* gray."

"It's *not.*"

"But it *does*" — he giggled — "it *does* look" — another spasm was rising, his voice was cracking, his nostrils were fluttering — "a little like — "

Salem's patience vanished with an exasperated "Ohhhh!" She snatched the dish away and stomped off to the kitchen. In a moment she stomped back and slammed a jar of bright yellow French's mustard onto the table. "*Here.*"

16

Salem glared at Eddie for a while, but he just went on blissfully chomping. She picked a piece of broccoli from the cold vegetable dish and scooped up some dip. "You should try this." He nodded and reached for another pig. Then he reached for the mints.

"Mints are for afterward," she told him. "They're the last thing you eat."

Eddie looked at her, looked at the mints in his hand. He started to put them back. She stopped him. "Oh, never mind. Go ahead." He didn't argue.

Eddie's crystal cup was still almost full. "What did you think of the punch?" she asked him.

He chewed for a second. "Mm," he nodded. "Good."

"I call it Periwinkle Punch. I just kind of like the way it sounds. Do you?"

Eddie had been scanning the toothpicks for the

plumpest pig. "What was it?" he said, making his choice.

"Periwinkle."

He dipped the pig into the French's yellow mustard, clamped it respectfully in his teeth, and drew it from the toothpick. "Yeah, neat."

"Want to know what goes into it?"

"Mm," he nodded, chewing. He really likes those pigs, Salem thought.

"Well, I can't tell you *exactly* what goes into it, because that's a chef's secret — me being the chef — but I can tell you there are five different kinds of fruit juice and two kinds of soda, plus the sherbet. I'll let you guess what kind of sherbet it is."

Eddie popped a pepperoni slice into his mouth. "Rainbow."

"That's right." Salem sunk a carrot into the dip. "But don't even *try* to guess what the other ingredients are."

"I won't."

"Because I wouldn't tell you if you were right, anyway. You know why?"

Eddie made a sandwich of two potato chips and a pepperoni slice. "Nope."

"Mystery," she said. "Mystery is the hidden ingredient. It's probably one of the reasons you like it so much. Mystery is supposed to make things appealing, because people are attracted to things they don't understand. You ever notice that?"

Eddie nodded, munching. "Mm."

Salem chewed on a broccoli stalk, thinking. "Yeah, me, too. Like when this kid came to my house last Halloween. I was already in for the night, so I answered the door, and there was the neatest costume I'd ever seen. I mean, I didn't have the foggiest idea *what* he was supposed to be. I didn't even know if it was a he. All I knew was I was fascinated by the costume, probably 'cause it wasn't like any other costume I ever saw. And then the person took off the mask — and it was Donald, my cousin from up the street. Zap" — she waved a carrot stick — "fascination gone."

She ladled herself some more punch. "C'mon, drink up, before I guzzle it all." His punch was still riding high in his cup. "You *sure* you like it?"

"Mm," said Eddie.

"Well, how come you're not drinking it?"

Eddie stopped chewing. He stared at her. He blinked. He stared at the cup. He picked up the cup. He looked into the cup. He raised the cup to his lips, closed his eyes, and drank it down in three fast, rather noisy swallows. He put the cup down. He couldn't seem to stop looking at it.

Salem started to giggle.

"What?" he said.

"You have a rainbow sherbet mustache."

While he wiped away his mustache, Salem ladled him another cupful of Periwinkle Punch.

"So anyway," she went on, "where was I?" She crunched a carrot stick. "Oh yeah — mystery. So . . . sometimes I read grown-up books and magazine stories, you know, so I can get a little preview of what I'm going to be reading when I'm in my twenties. And you know what one of the most mysterious things around is? You want to guess?"

Eddie scooped out the last of the onion dip with the last potato chip. "Uh — black holes?"

"Nope. Women." She studied his face for a reaction, but all she found was a mouth devouring another pig in a blanket. "Yep — women. Of course, we're not mysterious to ourselves. We're only mysterious to men. Men have a hard time figuring us out."

She cut the triangular tip off the wedge of brie. She worked the soft, almost gooey cheese in her mouth and closed her eyes, trying to glimpse a hint of mystery within herself. She opened her eyes, tilted her head. "Do you think I'm mysterious?"

Eddie looked at her. His face was a total blank. Had he continued to look at her for a thousand years, his face would still have been a total blank. "Never thought about it," he said at last.

Salem pulled up the hem of the pale yellow tablecloth till it covered her face below the eyes. "How about now?"

Eddie looked again. He shrugged. "A little, I guess."

"You sure? You're not just saying it?" She kept the veil up.

He picked a pig. "No, really."

"What exactly is it?" she persisted. "My eyes?" She leaned toward him, opening her eyes as wide as she could. If Eddie hadn't known better, he would have thought she was seeing a ghost. "When you look into them, do you feel yourself being drawn into the eternal mysteries of the female? Do you feel yourself falling in a bottomless void?"

He looked as directly as he could at her eyeballs. It was a little hard to focus, she being so close. The pig slid silently from its toothpick into his mouth. He nodded. "Uh-huh." Then burped.

A small wind of pepperoni, mustard, hot dog, onion, potato chip, and mint blew through the pale yellow veil. Salem backed into her chair and dropped the tablecloth. She did not have her notepad at hand, but she made a mental note on the many personalities of Eddie Mott:

4. Glutton

The mints were now as gone as the chips and dip. Three pepperonis lay on their plate like beefy half-dollars. The last of the pigs in a blanket was disappearing into Eddie's own bottomless void.

His cup was full.

"You hate the punch," she said.

His head snapped toward her. "No, really, I *like* it."

"All that stuff makes people thirsty. You should've drunk most of that bowl by now."

"I drank a lot before I came over today, that's all."

She got up. "I'll get you something you'll like. A nice old-fashioned Coke."

"No — " he called, but she was already in the kitchen.

She returned with a glassful. She set it in front of him. "Classic. Only the best."

He looked at it for a moment, then pushed it away. "Really," he said, "look." He grabbed the punch cup and downed it straight away. He wiped off his sherbet mustache and sucked it from his finger as he would a taffy. He closed his eyes and smiled. "Mmm."

Salem slumped into her chair, not sure if she had just won or lost.

The two talked for almost another hour. By the time Eddie left, most of the pickles were gone.

Salem was cleaning up the table when she happened to glance at the printed program. She gave the floor a crystal-tinkling stomp. "Drat!" They —

or at least she — had talked about everything *but* what they were *supposed* to talk about: a mascot for Plumstead.

Not wanting to be a pest, Salem waited until seven that evening to give Eddie a call. They could discuss it for five minutes over the phone; then at least they'd have something to report to Mr. Brimlow.

A woman's voice answered. Pleasant.

"Hello? Mrs. Mott?"

"Yes."

"This is Salem Brownmiller. Eddie's friend? He was over at my house this afternoon?"

"Oh, yes. How are you, Salem?"

"Fine, thank you. I was wondering if I could speak with Eddie."

There was a short delay before Mrs. Mott answered. "Oh, I'm sorry, Salem. Eddie's in bed. I'm afraid he's not feeling too well."

17

When Sunny Wyler arrived in homeroom Monday morning, a note was waiting for her:

Report to the principal's office.
AT ONCE!

Mr. Brimlow did not smile when she walked in. The hamster tank was on his desk. Besides the hamster, there was now a carpet of wood shavings and a plastic exercise wheel.

The principal said, "You were supposed to be here after school on Friday. Did you forget?"

She nodded. "Yeah."

"No," he said, "I don't think you forgot. I think, for some reason, you just want out of here, and you're doing everything you can to make me kick you out." He pointed at her nose. "Well, I have news for you, Sunshine. If you do *not* take care of this animal, I will make certain that you do *not* leave this school until your three years are up."

Outside, the notes of reveille signaled the flag's ascent. The principal and the sixth-grader stared at each other, Sunny wishing she had the nerve to tell him how much she hated being called Sunshine.

The principal held out a pair of books. "Here." She took them. "These are from our library. Read the parts about hamsters and how to care for them."

He pointed to a shopping bag in the corner. "There's everything you'll need. Food. Wood chips. I'm going to set it up on a table right outside the office. This will be everybody's pet. And you will be the petkeeper. Every day. After school. Here. Got it?"

She nodded.

"Okay, on your way."

Sunny wandered off to first period wishing Hillary were there to talk to about this. What exactly did he mean? He had said he would not kick her out if she did not take care of the beast. Did that mean he definitely *would* kick her out if she did? Did that mean she did not even have to be bad anymore?

By third period music, she decided she couldn't afford to take that chance. She would take care of the beast *and* continue to be bad. She would leave the principal no choice.

On this day Lips Hummelsdorf began actual preparations for the assembly presentation. He spent time with each group of instruments, working on their notes. The rubber band section, for example, was fifteen strong. Though the rubber bands were huge, each one by itself made only a puny twitter. But a whole chorus of them, said Lips, would be another story. The audience would hear a twang they wouldn't soon forget. The secret was to pluck them all at precisely the same instant.

On this first day of practice, the twangers were decidedly ragged. As was every other group. Salem's drum section sounded like furniture falling down stairs. And together, Eddie and his trombone-mates sounded like a herd of constipated cows.

There was only one cymbalist — Sunny Wyler. When Hummelsdorf walked right past her to the buckets and spoons, you could almost hear the class gasp in amazement. After what had happened at the last class, they had expected a confrontation at least; maybe, if they were lucky, an all-out fistfight.

And then, when the period was over and Lips called, "Cymbals player, stay a minute," half the class found reasons to hang around the hallway just outside. But Lips closed the door.

"You don't like it here, do you?" he said.

Sunny shrugged.

"Sometimes I don't, either. Especially with all this blame coming down on me now, and they leave me with all the oldest instruments." For once, Sunny found herself staring at a puss as sour as her own. "So," he went on, "you say you won't play the cymbals, and I say I won't let you be the only student not in the band that day. What are we going to do?"

Sunny shrugged.

"Will you play something else? Rubber band?"

"No."

"Bucket?"

"No."

He stared at her. "What's your name?"

"Wyler."

"First."

"Sunny."

His eyebrows shot up. "*Sunny?* You sure it's not Cloudy?"

She let her glare be her answer.

He sat back. He gave a what-did-I-do-to-deserve-this sigh, which pushed out his lower lip even more. Sunny wondered if it was true, that you could see your reflection in it. It *was* shiny.

"Okay then," he said, "if you won't play anything, you can't be on the stage. But you also can't be in the audience. I will *not* have you make a mockery of me by being the only student in the audience. So you know what that means, Wyler?"

"No."

"That means you'll be sick that afternoon. You'll have to go see the nurse, stay in the infirmary. You won't show up. Agreed?"

Sunny was about to say okay, but then she thought: Hey, wait a minute, why should I agree? If the last thing he wants is for me to be in the audience, then that's exactly what I *should* do. So she said, "I don't feel sick."

"Well," he said, "it's almost two weeks away. That's plenty of time to suddenly come down with a nice stomachache."

"I don't get stomachaches."

"Well, *get* one."

"That would be lying."

Sunny then saw the last thing she expected: Mr. Hummelsdorf laughing. It seemed like he laughed forever. She was glad the door was shut. When he finished, he shook his head and looked at her as if he actually liked her.

"I'm old," he said. "I don't need this. I used to think, by now I'd be directing a major college band. Michigan State. Oklahoma. Two hundred members." He wagged his head. "Are you always this belligerent?"

"Huh?"

"A pain. Are you always such a pain?"

"No," she said. "I used to be good. I just started being a pain when I came here. I think I must be allergic to this school."

That set him off laughing again. "Oh, my . . .

okay, here — " He scribbled out a late note for her next class. "Maybe I *do* need this," he chuckled as he sent her on her way.

Eddie Mott had hoped to avoid Salem at lunch that day, but there was the voice that could only be hers, behind him: "Hey, Eddie, wait up."

Maybe he could draw her attention away. He said, as she caught up to him, "What do you think Lips said to Sunny in there today?" In spite of his mood, it made him feel a tiny bit bad and a tiny bit older to call a teacher "Lips."

Salem grinned deliciously. "I don't know. Wish I were a bug on the wall."

Before he could say anything else, she spotted the absence. "Hey, where's your lunch bag?"

He shrugged. "Uh . . . I'm buying today."

One glance at his face and she knew. She made him stop just inside the door of the cafeteria. "No, you're not. It got stolen, didn't it?"

He stared at her with what he hoped was his best I-haven't-the-slightest-idea-what-you're-talking-about face. "No," he said.

"That nickelhead jerk, right? He got you when Pickles wasn't around, and this time he took your whole lunch."

Eddie's eyes began to itch. "No, I'm buying today." *Don't look down*, he pleaded silently. *Please.*

She looked down. "Oh, no."

He had tried to wipe the pudding off in the bathroom, but you could still see traces of chocolate between his sneaker laces.

She looked back up. "He did to you what Pickles did to him."

Eddie tried to stare at her, but he couldn't. What a curse! To be a kid and not be able to tell a convincing lie. His mother said he wore his heart on his sleeve, whatever that meant. All he knew was that the whole world always seemed to know what he was feeling inside.

Salem stared at him until he blinked, then slumped, and she knew that she had gone too far.

She steered him toward the nearest table. They sat down. Half the school was mobbing past them for the lunch lines.

"I'm sorry," she said.

He shook his head. He stared down at his balled fist. "I'm a wimp."

"No — "

"I'm the world's biggest wimp."

"Eddie, you're only a sixth-grader." She touched his arm. He jerked it away.

"They throw me around like a football. They spit on me. They steal my lunch. They drop pudding on my shoe . . . and I don't do *nothin'*. And on toppa all that, I can't even *lie* right. What kinda kid *am* I? I know that story you're writing is about me. You can call it 'Eddie the Wimp.' I'm *worse* than a wimp. I'm a *disgrace*."

Kids going by were staring. A few eighth-graders snickered.

Salem's left hand had been resting in her book bag, touching her notepad. Suddenly she felt crummy. She now saw that in her own way, she, too, had mistreated him. She had tried to divide him into so many personalities. She had tried to reduce him to pages in a notepad. How insulting to him. Eddie Mott was not a subplot, as Mr. Brimlow would say, or even a main plot. He was a person. He was her friend.

18

This time T. Charles Brimlow was properly ready for lunch. He had brought a tablecloth from home and his hand-carved, hand-painted wooden dandelion to serve as a centerpiece. For the sake of easy cleanup, the plates, cups, and utensils were paper and plastic, but they were best quality and coordinated nicely with the tablecloth. He even felt a little proud when Salem entered, looked the table over, and pronounced it *"verrry* nice."

As the others came in, he updated his mental files.

Eddie Mott: faithful, competent flag-raiser; still looks like he wants to disappear, except when he's looking at Sunny Wyler.

Elizabeth Sunshine Wyler: still the sullen face and DEATH TO MUSHROOMS T-shirt; problems with Maestro Hummelsdorf; hair — did she dunk it in molasses?

Dennis Johnson: the pickle boy, as Mrs. Wilburham calls him, is a patriot; hasn't missed a morning blowing reveille.

He waited till they had been served before addressing them.

"First of all, I'm going to give you an official name — the Principal's Posse." They seemed to approve. "Now, schoolwise, it looks like we're on our way. We just finished our shakedown cruise. One week, and we didn't sink. I think we're going to make it."

He turned to Salem. "So, do we have a nominee for mascot yet?"

Miss Brownmiller briefly glossed over a mention that she had forgotten to convene a meeting — shifting eyes told Mr. Brimlow this wasn't quite true — and went on to offer her own views on the subject. "Whatever we nominate, let's not pick wildcats. Or lions or bears or dragons. For one thing, they're so common. Everybody has them. And for another thing, they're all, like, violent and . . . *growly*. Why does a mascot have to be a flesh-eating carnivore? Why can't it be something more original?"

She stopped, waited. The principal knew a cue when he heard one. "For example?" he said.

Salem waved her hand. "Oh . . . vegetables."

Eddie Mott sprang to life. "The Plumstead *Onions!*"

Everybody laughed, even Sunny Wyler.

Suggestions flew, laughter grew.

"The Plumstead String Beans!"

"The Plumstead Cauliflowers!"

"The Plumstead Plums!"

"Pancakes!"

"Bran Muffins!"

"Buttonholes!"

"Hamsters!"

Everyone stopped. For the first time in two lunches, Sunny Wyler had voluntarily spoken. All eyes swung to her.

Mr. Brimlow whispered it: "Hamsters." He pronounced it louder, his head tilted, testing, tasting the sound of it: "Plumstead Hamsters." He looked around the table, his eyes bright: "The . . . Plumstead . . . *Hamsters*."

"I love it!" chirped Salem.

"Shall we vote?" said Mr. Brimlow.

"Yeah!" came several voices.

"Okay, Posse, all in favor of the sixth-grade nominee for school mascot being the Hamsters, say 'Aye.' "

"Aye!"

"Opposed, 'No.' "

Silence.

"Hamsters it is!"

Cheers and slaps on the back to Sunny Wyler, whose face had regained its usual pout.

That day, Wednesday, was clean-the-hamster-house day. Sunny went to the lobby later than usual. She wanted to be sure no kids were still around to see her do the dirty work.

From the main office, where Mr. Brimlow had left them, she got the newspapers, paper bag, rag, and tennis ball can. Before today, she really hadn't had much to do with the animal. She just dumped some food in and, once, filled the water bottle. She never even really looked at it, except when she reached down to put the pellets in the bowl and found the animal looking up at her. She had yanked her arm out, fearing the beast had a mind to scurry up her sleeve. But she kept thinking of those pure black shiny eyes, so big. She had been remembering those eyes when *"Hamster!"* popped unexpectedly from her mouth at lunch a couple hours earlier.

She took off the screen that served as the cover of the glass tank. She reached in and took out the exercise wheel, food bowl, salt wheel, and water bottle. Now, the animal itself. It had to be removed so she could clean the tank. That's what the tennis ball can was for, so said one of the books she had read.

She removed the cap from the can and laid the can on the floor of the tank. Sure enough, within seconds, the animal went sniffing into it, exploring this new piece of furniture. Sunny clamped the cap on the can, lifted it out, and set it on the floor. Mr. Brimlow had punched an air hole in the cap.

She then proceeded to dump the old wood shavings onto the newspaper, which in turn she folded and stashed in the paper bag. She cleaned the inside of the tank with a rag, dumped in new shavings, replaced the furniture, and finally, holding the opened tennis can at a sliding board angle, dumped the animal back home.

Suddenly the beast stood on its hind legs, its paws on the glass walls. Was it going to leap? Quickly, she replaced the screen. In less than two minutes she was on her way home.

"So," Hillary asked that night, "is it a boy or girl hamster?"

"A boy," said Sunny.

"How do you know?"

"Some science teacher said."

"So who's gonna take care of it when you're gone, after you get kicked out?"

Sunny snapped, "I don't *know*. I don't *care*. I hate that . . . *rodent*."

Hillary scowled back. "Well, don't go hollering at me. *I* didn't make you take care of the thing. Look at my hair." She grabbed a handful on top of her head and pulled it up straight. When she released it, it stayed up: a thin, greasy, hairy, foot-tall spike.

Sunny laughed.

"Yeah, laugh," growled Hillary. "My father laughs, too. He says it looks like string cheese.

My sister says seaweed. My mother's ready to kill me. I keep telling her it's *not* grease, it's *mousse*. I tell her it's my new style. Every night I come out of the shower with a towel around my head and pretend I just washed my hair. You gotta get kicked out soon!"

Sunny pulled her own hair into spikes, till her head resembled a medieval weapon. "See — you're not the only one. I'm working on it."

"Well, you better work faster." Hillary scratched her head furiously. "I'm itching like mad. I think I already have cooties."

"C'mere," said Sunny. She led Hillary to her dresser. "Kneel down." The two girls knelt in front of the dresser. "Ready?"

"Ready for what?"

Sunny grinned faintly and opened the bottom drawer. Hillary, unaware that Sunny was holding her breath, peered into the drawer, but it was not her eyes but what reached her nose that knocked her backward as smartly as if she had been punched. *"EEEWW!"* she shrieked, clamping her hand over her face and gagging, scrambling to the farthest corner of the room.

Sunny closed the drawer, moved away, took a small breath.

"What — ?" gasped Hillary.

"My socks. I've been wearing them for a week now. I keep them in their cage here, by themselves. I moved everything else out."

Hillary, pinching her nose, oinked, "How can you *stand* it?"

"I hold my breath and put on my shoes *real* fast." Sunny grinned as she peeked into the future. "Any day now . . . "

19

Principal Brimlow made the announcement next morning: "We now have the candidates for school mascot. Eighth-grade nominee is . . . the Demons! Seventh-grade nominee is . . . the Wildcats! Sixth-graders nominate . . . the Hamsters! We will vote next Thursday. The winner will be announced the following day during opening assembly."

By lunchtime every sixth-grader in Plumstead Middle School had managed to stop by the hamster house and say hello. The greeting usually took the form of a fingernail tapping upon the glass wall and waking up the occupant, who was trying to take a nap. The result was a hundred happy sixth-graders and one very cranky hamster, who profoundly wished that one of those tapping fingertips would come within reach of his teeth.

Sometime, somehow, during the day, the hamster also acquired a name: Humphrey.

By the following week, Sunny Wyler found herself longing for the "old days," when it was just her and the hamster after school. Now, when she came to feed him, he was in such a foul mood from being kept awake by tapping fingernails all day, he was no fun at all to be with. "What a grouch," she muttered to him every day.

Sometimes when she arrived after school, she found food on the table on which the hamster house rested. Left by well-meaning sixth-graders, the food was usually unhealthy for hamsters: M&M's, brownies, pickle chips, raviolis.

Sometimes, too, she found things that were more than unhealthy: bubble gum, old soap, dirty erasers. These things, Sunny knew, were from some seventh- and eighth-graders, kids who wanted the mascot to be a demon or a wildcat. Once, in fact, she found a sign propped in front of the tank:

MENU FOR THURSDAY
HAM(STER)BURGER

Thursday was the day of the vote. Sunny ripped the sign in half. She ripped the pieces again and kept ripping in frustration and anger. She was mad at the hamster for being so cute. Mad at herself for having feelings for it. Mad at the principal for not kicking her out. And mad at the whole school for butting in between her and Hillary.

She threw the pieces, practically confetti now, into a basket. She would have to make her move soon.

20

For the most part, Lips Hummelsdorf was satisfied, even pleased. Counting today, Wednesday, only two days of practice remained, and yet he felt confident they would do it.

The rubber bands were lagging, but he would have them up to speed by Friday. The washboards and drums were coming along. The kazoos were better than expected, and the buckets and spoons — well — they lent his music a surprisingly primitive power.

Only one question remained: Would he become the first bandmaster to direct a whole school — or a whole school minus one?

Miss Wyler. She of the sunny disposition. She was still refusing to bang the cymbals and still threatening to be the only student in the audience. He feared she meant it.

As he worked with the soda bottlists that day, coaxing a mournful, flutelike note from them, he noticed that Miss Wyler was not only her usual sullen self today, she was also something of an island. The chairs directly before and behind her and the chair to her left were all unoccupied. Only the Mott boy, a trombonist, sat near her.

Within the next minute, two students slipped away into seats even farther from her. Below the bottlists' note, he sensed an undercurrent of whispers, from which erupted an occasional cough or muffled squawk. Another student moved. Something like a tide was receding from Wyler. Suddenly a kazooist popped up and staggered to the back of the room, his hands to his face.

Hummelsdorf wandered a step into the now vacated space around Wyler and Mott, and he knew. And then he knew why — her shoes were off. And he knew, without asking, that it wasn't for lack of soap. It was deliberate.

She had won.

"Wyler," he thundered, "out! Principal's office! Now!"

Sunny padded down the hallways in her stocking feet, holding her breath as best she could, taking in air through her mouth, in tiny sips. Along the way one teacher, two teachers, left their blackboards, took a look, took a whiff, and shut their classroom doors. Later that day, a number of students would report to their parents that a skunk had been loose in the school.

As Sunny approached the office, she slowed

down. The hamster house . . . something was different . . . *wrong*. She rushed up to it. The screen was off, leaning against the tank.

The hamster — Humphrey — was gone!

Moments later, Sunny was in the office, hysterically telling Mrs. Wilburham and Mr. Brimlow what had happened. They hurried out to see for themselves, leaving Sunny alone in the office. She looked down. Her shoes were on her feet. She could not remember putting them on.

The principal made announcements. He wasn't after punishment, he said. If you took the hamster, just put it back in the tank when no one was looking. No questions asked.

Accusations flew. Sixth-graders accused seventh-graders of hamsternapping. Seventh-graders accused eighth-graders. Everyone accused the nickelheads. The nickelheads gestured innocently and pointed out that the animal itself could have nudged the cover off and climbed out.

The usual Wednesday lunch meeting of the Principal's Posse was replaced by a schoolwide search.

In the cafeteria that day, several sixth-graders, recalling the sign propped in front of the tank, looked at their hamburgers and screamed.

After school, Sunny gave the tank its usual

Wednesday cleaning. There was no need for the tennis ball can.

Tears came to her eyes as she looked at the lobby wall above the tank. A sixth-grade English class had taped a dozen sheets of paper together to make a banner. It read:

HUMPHREY — COME HOME!

The school was locked up and closed down at nine that night. The hamster house was still empty.

21

Mrs. Wilburham took her job as school secretary quite seriously. She had her own key and usually opened up the building before the custodians arrived.

Thursday morning was no exception. Upon arriving, she turned on the coffee maker in the teachers' lounge and headed for the kitchen. On the side of one shelf in the big stainless-steel food freezer she kept her frozen muffins. With boxes of blueberry, corn, and bran, she looked forward each morning to her tasty dilemma: which flavor to choose.

Some days she could not make up her mind until she took each package off the shelf and studied the pictures of the muffins within. This was one of those days.

First she took the bran muffin package from the shelf and considered it. Then the corn. Then the blueberry. So intent was she on the muffins that at first she failed to notice the hamster. It was on

116

the shelf below the muffins and more to the center of the freezer. It was lying on a box of twenty-four Mister Mario's Delux cheese pizzas. It was on its back, its four legs straight in the air. Its eyes were closed. It wasn't moving.

Blueberry, decided Mrs. Wilburham. She removed a single muffin and replaced all three boxes. That's when she saw it. She screeched, thinking it was a mouse. Then she realized it was the hamster. What was its name? Hubert? Harry? Mrs. Wilburham never had cared much for this hamster business. This one was either dead or it was impersonating a dead cockroach. With a corner of the blueberry muffin box, she nudged one of the stiff, upraised legs. The beast rolled onto its side like a wooden toy.

What to do with a dead hamster in the food freezer? First, close the door, you're wasting electricity. She shut the door. But she knew she couldn't leave it in the freezer one second longer than necessary. Suppose the dietician came in early today. Suppose the Board of Health dropped by. Suppose the beast had romped around the freezer going to the bathroom before it died. Suppose there were little frozen hamster pooplets all over. Suppose . . . she looked at the muffin in her hand . . . of *course* they were blueberries. Nevertheless, she tossed the muffin into a trash can.

She searched through the utensil bin and came up with the largest spatula she could find, a real he-man pancake flipper. She pulled the trash can in close. She reopened the freezer, scanned the interior — good, no pooplets. Carefully, as if she were turning a fried egg, she slid the spatula under the corpse. Her plan was to dump it into the trash can, cover it with papers — get it out of sight — then wait for Mr. Brimlow, and tell him.

Slowly, carefully, she lifted the spatula. As the body rose on the silvery surface, it gave the impression of a tiny, vanquished warrior borne from some arena of combat on its shield. Swinging the spatula around toward the trash can brought the front end of the animal into view. She saw the frost then, a white dusting on the animal's nose and whiskers and closed eyes, as though it had been sniffing powdered sugar when it expired.

Mrs. Wilburham's heart sank. This was not, after all, a half-eaten hot dog. It was not garbage.

She placed the body back on the box of Mario's pizzas, shut the freezer door, and hurried back to the office. To her delight, she saw the pickle boy waiting by himself outside the front door. She let him in.

22

Pickles took it from there. He retrieved the body from the freezer. He found a box of pencils in the office. He emptied out the pencils. From the infirmary he obtained cotton balls. He pulled them shapeless and laid them together in the bottom of the pencil box, making a soft, white bedding. Upon the bedding he placed the body. He then set the box next to the glass tank in the lobby. He did not disturb the tank or the empty exercise wheel.

He completed this by the time Mr. Brimlow arrived. Pickles related to the principal what had happened.

Buses began to pull up. Students crowded outside the door, awaiting the bell. Those in front peered in, making a bridge between the dark glass and their eyes.

When the students poured in, they found the hamster lying in state and Pickles Johnson at rigid attention by the casket. There were cries of surprise and grief as the students paused, then moved on.

With everyone in homeroom, the principal called for a moment of silence. In the farthest reaches of the school, from the teachers' lounge to the cafeteria kitchen, could be heard a bugle playing taps.

Motorists on their way to work slowed down to 15 m.p.h. and wondered why the Plumstead Middle School flag was flying half-mast.

All day long students went to classes by way of the lobby. Not just sixth-graders, but many seventh- and eighth-graders as well.

The votes for school mascot were cast and collected in homeroom after last period. The ballots were brought to the main office.

Upon leaving school, few of the students were surprised to find the casket empty. They asked among themselves where he was buried. No one seemed to know. Nearly everyone called him Humphrey now. Seldom was he referred to as "the hamster."

Among the last to leave the lobby that day were Salem Brownmiller and Eddie Mott and Sunny Wyler and Pickles Johnson.

For quite a while, no one said a word. Then Sunny cleared her throat and spoke to Pickles. "Did you bury him?"

Pickles turned, his eyes wide. "No, didn't you?"

23

Seated onstage along with the principal and other school administrators, Maestro Hummelsdorf tapped his baton nervously on the side of his chair. His hands were clammy.

Had he bitten off too much? Was he about to make a fool of himself? For the past two weeks he had rehearsed the students as much as he could in their separate music periods. For the most part, they had learned their limited parts well. But not once had they practiced together, all 340 of them. This time, following the announcement of the mascot, would be the first.

Would they follow his directions? Would he prove that a whole school, musicians or not, could perform as a band? Would it in fact *be* the whole school, all 340 of them? Or 339?

He scanned the auditorium for Wyler, but could not locate her. Backstage, behind the curtain, the cymbals sat alongside the other instruments. The clash of the cymbals would bracket his tuba solo, which would be followed by the Johnson boy playing reveille — a late addition to the score. Reveille: wake up: a new beginning: a new school year: a new school! The perfect finale. He loved it.

Would they?

"... and the winner *is* ... " the principal was saying, holding up a slip of paper, "... the Plumstead ... *Hamsters!*"

The place went wild. The little sixth-graders were joined by older ones yelping and jumping in their seats. Obviously, it was a sentimental choice, a memorial to the dead. Who knows how many votes the animal piled up just by croaking?

Personally, Hummelsdorf detested the choice. Marching bands tended to take on the names of their schools' mascots. He cringed at the thought of the Strawberry Festival parade next spring ... someone at a microphone announcing as they passed the review stand: "... and here they come, ladies and gentlemen ... the famous Plumstead Middle School Mmmmarching *Hammmmmmmsters!*"

And now the principal was saying it's time for the music, and the curtain was whooshing open, and the audience was getting up. While the principal and other assembly speakers pulled their chairs from the stage, Hummelsdorf took his place at the podium front and center. Only scattered teachers remained in the seats now, as the students poured down the aisles and out to the wings. He felt a small surge of power.

He turned to face the students clomping onto the stage. He had given them all diagrams, so they knew where to stand or sit. All instruments waited except for the whistles and rubber bands, which were supposed to be in their players' pockets.

Hummelsdorf turned to the auditorium, seeking and again failing to find Wyler. When he turned back, he almost jumped. There she was, in front, a few feet to his left, holding the cymbals by her sides, as he had shown her. She wore a different shirt, and a different face. Her hair looked . . . normal.

The students were testing their instruments, producing a jumbled junkyard of toots, tweets, bams, and twangs. The maestro mounted the single step. He tapped his baton on the podium. The band fell silent.

Hummelsdorf stood as erect as his hunched, five-feet-four-inch frame would allow. Whenever he stood at the podium, all those eyes looking up, waiting for him, he felt he was the tallest person in the world. He raised his arms. At his back, the vast, expectant stillness swelled like a balloon to the bursting point.

He turned to the twenty whistles. "Ready," he mouthed silently, and prayed they were. He

brought the baton down. Twenty whistles —
well, nineteen — tweeted in unison, four quick
notes. They were off!

For the first time Hummelsdorf was hearing
what before he had only imagined in his inner ear.
He was pleased, even surprised. By Beethoven,
this wasn't bad! Even his defective hearing could
tell that. Sure, it was jangling and raucous, but
in a quirky sort of way. Sure, it was amateurish,
but in an honest, genuine sort of way. The dueling
kazoos and soda bottles. The primitively happy
clamor of the buckets and spoons. The washboards' stirring racket that made him want to
march. The perfectly comical *TWANG!* of the rubber bands. Behind him he thought he heard out-
bursts of laughter and clapping. In his band's faces
he saw the approval of the audience. Maybe they
weren't the Philharmonic, but they were enter-
taining.

The last part was coming up. He nodded to
Wyler. She brought the cymbals up from her
sides, her eyes fixed on his. With a brisk down-
beat, he snapped off the washboards' final roll.
His arms aloft, he held the silence — he held the
world — for one second . . . two . . . three . . .
he turned full face to Wyler and gave the down-
beat a sledgehammer blow. Wyler's hands leaped
together, letting the force of the collision drive
them apart, turning the cymbals outward, like a
broad brass-petaled flower, letting the sound

bloom over the auditorium. *Just as he had taught her.*

Almost forgetting himself, he laid down the baton and took up his tuba. He worked his lips briefly, cleared his throat, took a deep breath, and blew. The first thing that came out was a strangulated belch of a note such as Hummelsdorf had never heard, much less produced, before. The second thing was a hamster.

"Humphrey!" cried several voices as the animal clung momentarily to the tuba's massive rim, then dropped to the stage floor.

"Rodent!" bawled a voice from the audience, and a dozen teachers screamed and jumped onto their seats.

The stage was in tumult: 340 band members and one conductor lunging and shrieking at once.

"There he is!"

"There!"

"There!"

"Stuff your pants in your socks! They crawl up legs!"

"EEEEEEEEEEEE!"

Chairs clattered, buckets clanged. Who was chasing whom, it was hard to tell. So loud was the commotion that no one heard when Sunny Wyler started screaming: "Stand *still*! You'll *step* on him!"

The tumult was fully into its third minute and Sunny still screaming in vain when Eddie Mott came up to her, grinning as usual. One hand covered the mouth of his trombone.

"I stuck it in front of him," he said, "and he scooted right in."

Gaping in disbelief, Sunny meekly obeyed when he said, "Put your hand over mine." He pulled his hand away, leaving hers to cover the trombone.

"They have it!" someone shouted. "Look!"

The commotion ceased. All eyes turned toward the sixth-grade girl holding the trombone.

Eddie nodded. "Go ahead."

Carefully Sunny reached into the mouth of the instrument. When she withdrew with a tiny, furry, caramel-colored bundle in her fingers, a full-school cheer erupted from the stage. And for the first time since she had arrived at Plumstead, looking straight at Eddie Mott, no less, Sunny smiled.

Along with chants of "Humphrey! Humphrey!" the notes of reveille filled the auditorium.

24

"It's like . . . hibernation, I guess," Sunny was explaining to Hillary that night. "When the temperature goes below forty-something, they go into this kind of coma. Their heart only beats about once a minute. It's just like they're dead. So it must've thawed out and woke up and climbed out of its own coffin."

"And into a *tuba*?" marveled Hillary, pulling a brush again and again through her newly washed hair.

"Yeah," chuckled Sunny. "You shoulda seen the conductor's face when he heard his first note."

"So how did the hamster get in the freezer in the first place?"

Sunny shrugged. "Who knows? Probably some jerk eighth-grader."

There was a minute of silence.

"So now you're gonna stay."

Sunny looked away from her friend. She picked up her own brush and began stroking her hair. She nodded. "I guess."

Hillary walked around the room, touching things. She went to the bedroom window and stood there, looking out.

She did not see Sunny pull off her shoes, then her socks. She did not know Sunny was sneaking up behind her, reaching over her shoulder, until she saw the socks dangling in front of her nose. She screamed, flailed at the socks, and steam-rollered over Sunny on her way to the closet.

Sunny followed, bent with laughter. At the closet entrance, she extended the socks into the darkness. "Hillary, here, take a whiff."

"No!"

"Hill, come on. Just a little one. You'll live, I promise."

From the darkness came a short sniff; then another, longer one; then a long, deep breath. A hand snatched the socks. Hillary came out, grinning.

"It's better if I'm happy at my school, right?" said Sunny.

"Right," agreed Hillary, breathing deeply. "Right!"

On Saturday morning Eddie Mott watched only half his usual dose of cartoons. He turned off the TV and went outside, looking for someone to play with. He walked one block, two blocks. A few grown-ups were outside doing chores, but not a kid in sight. Cartooning, Eddie figured.

He was ready to give up when he heard the sound of a skateboard clacking down the sidewalk cracks behind him. Then a voice calling: "Yo, Mott!"

He turned just as Pickles Johnson wrapped him with a curl-and-stop.

"Hi," said Eddie, staring at the pickleboard. He had never been this close to it.

"What's up?" said Pickles.

Eddie shrugged. "Not much. Nobody's out."

Pickles spread his arms. "Hey — do I look like nobody?"

Eddie laughed.

Pickles pushed the pickleboard over to Eddie. "Try it."

Eddie goggled. "You kiddin'?"

"No, go ahead, step on."

"I might crash it."

"You won't. It's a tank."

"I'm not a good skateboarder."

Pickles lifted Eddie's right foot and set it on the board. *"Go!"*

Eddie went.

He couldn't believe he was actually riding the famous pickleboard. It was much larger than he had realized. It was like riding a giant green slipper. And smooth — wow! — it took the ground like whipped cream melting over his tongue.

The sidewalk was level here. Eddie coasted easily along while Pickles trotted at his side.

"Waddaya think?" said Pickles.

"Wow!" was all Eddie could answer.

They went along like that for a block or so; then Pickles hopped aboard in front of Eddie and said, "Pull your foot in and *hang on!*" Eddie grabbed onto Pickles' waist, and away they went on a rollicking ride. Eddie couldn't have been prouder if he had hitched a ride on Superman's cape.

Ten minutes later, in a neighborhood Eddie did not recognize, Pickles swung up a driveway and into a backyard. "My house," he said. He parked the pickleboard. "Come on. I have something to show you."

Pickles steered Eddie down a set of steps into a basement. "This is my workbench," he said, pointing to a long wooden table busy with tools, containers, and scraps of every sort. He led Eddie to the end of the bench, where he picked up an old jelly jar. It was half full of a greenish-gray goop.

"Ugh," said Eddie. "What *is* it?"

"Mashed garbage," said Pickles, "mixed with rotten milk and dead fish juice." He held out the jar. "Want a taste?"

Eddie jumped back.

"I don't blame you. It could be fatal. The secret is the fish juice. My father uses it to fertilize his tomato plants in the spring."

"So what's it for?" said Eddie.

Pickles gazed proudly at the goop. "Anti-nickelhead booby trap."

"*What?*"

"They attacked your lunch two times so far, right?"

"Right."

"So, as soon as I get this all worked out, you can have a surprise ready for them next time. I have to figure out something to put the stuff in. I'm thinking about a Rice Krispie bar." Pickles' eyes were bright as he explained. "Cut it in half. Hollow out the middle. Put in the stuff. Stick the two halves back together. You take it to school each day. Nickelhead swipes your lunch. Nickelhead bites into Rice Krispie bar. Nickelhead — "

They finished it together: "*dies!*"

"Or thinks he's gonna," grinned Pickles. "And that's the last time anybody ever takes *your* lunch."

They laughed. Eddie was almost giddy. First a ride on the pickleboard, and now this. Who would have thought Pickles Johnson would one day turn his genius on Eddie Mott?

And that's what touched Eddie most of all — not the anti-nickelhead booby trap itself, but the fact that Pickles had done it for him. Eddie knew then that Pickles had become more than a flag-raising partner or lunch-bag rescuer. He was a new friend.

25

As far as Eddie knew, there was no mail delivery on Sunday, so what was a white envelope doing in the mailbox? He took it out. There was no stamp, no address even. Only his name.

He took it up to his room and opened it. There were three sheets of paper, stapled together in the upper left corner, typewritten. Or maybe computer printed. At the top it said:

The Wimp Who Wasn't
by
Salem Jane Brownmiller

He let it fall to his bed. He closed his door. He got out his mini-basketball set and fired up about fifty three-pointers. He dropkicked the nearly weightless, foam ball into his closet. He returned to the bed. He sat down, picked up the papers, and began to read.

It was a story. About a kid named Perry T.

Winkle. This kid has all kinds of problems as a new sixth-grader in middle school.

After being flung around by some big football players on the way to school, he refuses to leave the bus until the principal coaxes him off. Everywhere he turns — bathroom, cafeteria, hallways — he gets terrorized by eighth-graders.

The kid, Perry, soon gets disgusted with himself. "I'm a wimp!" he cries out. He believes he has no guts. He wants to stay in bed forever. He doesn't deserve to appear in public. He's nothing but a human beanbag.

And then Perry goes to a girl's house for lunch. Her name is Susan, and she serves him all this good stuff to eat. But there's one thing that isn't good: her homemade punch. In fact, it's abominable. But Susan thinks her punch is great, and she keeps pestering him to drink more, *more*.

Well, the thing about Perry is, he's a good-hearted kid. He sees how proud Susan is of her punch, and he doesn't want to hurt her feelings. So he keeps drinking it, and what's more, pretending he likes it.

He goes home and gets sick. When Susan finds out, she tells herself it's because of all the food he ate. But deep inside, she knows better. It was the punch. And now she realizes that he sacrificed himself for her feelings.

In the end Susan sits in her room wondering how she can thank Perry. And wondering how she can convince him that he's not a wimp at all, but in his own little way, he's a hero.

Eddie just sat there for a while. Then he put the story away in his special drawer where he kept his most valuable stuff. He went back to shooting mini-ball baskets.

He thought about his first horrifying days at Plumstead Middle School: flung around the bus, nickelheads after his lunch, spit at, lost. He shuddered just to remember. Then he thought of recent days: catching the hamster, Sunny Wyler smiling at him, Pickles' friendship, Salem's story.

It suddenly occurred to Eddie that something was missing, had been missing for several days now. He no longer wished he were back in grade school. In fact . . . he looked at his clock. It said 3 P.M. That would be nine . . . plus seven . . . sixteen hours and fifteen minutes till he would catch the bus to school next day.

He couldn't wait.

About the Author

Jerry Spinelli was born in Norristown, Pennsylvania. He attended Gettysburg College and The Writing Seminars at Johns Hopkins University. His novels include *Maniac Magee*, which won the Newbery Medal, *Who Put That Hair in My Toothbrush?*, *Space Station Seventh Grade*, *Jason and Marceline*, and *Dump Days*. He lives in Phoenixville, Pennsylvania, with his wife and fellow author, Eileen Spinelli, and sons Sean and Ben, both of whom are safely past sixth grade.